MK

"What do y
Alannah a

"You," he sa

Surprisingly the softly delivered
monosyllable did not astonish her.

"Exactly how?" she asked.

"As my wife."

This time her eyes flew to his face.
Involuntarily she shivered. "To take
the place of the one I killed?"

"Exactly." When Alannah said nothing
he continued. "And to supply me
with the child you killed, too."

It was stupid to be so afraid that her
brain refused to function. Of course
he could not force her to marry him.

A long moment passed before he
said, "You owe me, Alannah, and
for once in your life you're going to
pay. I don't want love or affection or
companionship. I don't want
anything from you but the use of
your body, and that I will have."

ROBYN DONALD

the guarded heart

Harlequin Books

TORONTO • NEW YORK • LONDON
AMSTERDAM • PARIS • SYDNEY • HAMBURG
STOCKHOLM • ATHENS • TOKYO • MILAN

Harlequin Presents first edition September 1983
ISBN 0-373-10623-8

Original hardcover edition published in 1983
by Mills & Boon Limited

CHAPTER ONE

THE big jet swooped over the Southern Alps, clear in the antipodean autumn, the eternal snows a beacon to at least one passenger.

Alannah Finderne turned to the charming American widow beside her and told her excitedly, 'One of those peaks is probably Mount Cook, the highest mountain in New Zealand, but I can't tell you which one! I've seen them on the horizon all my life, but they look so different from this angle.'

'They look beautiful,' Mrs Hamel said softly. 'Nearly home, honey. Will your mother and your sister be meeting you?'

'I hope so. Trina is still at school, of course—no, no, she's not. She finished at the end of last year. This year she's at university doing a year's pre-med and then next year she'll start learning to be a doctor.'

Mrs Hamel smiled, her warm brown eyes sympathetic as they rested on the vivid, irregular features of the girl who had intuitively divined the nervousness of her fellow passenger and set aside her inbuilt reserve to ease it with conversation.

'You sound so confident,' she said quietly. 'In the States it's a difficult course.'

'Oh, Trina is brilliant.' Alannah's voice was casual, totally without envy. 'I mean, really brilliant. She'll have no trouble. She has a real vocation. We've always known that Trina would go in for medicine.'

'And you?'

For some reason a flush ran through the pale matt skin.

'Oh, I want to go to university, too,' Alannah said airily. 'I'm very interested in computers.'

'Your parents must be proud of such clever girls. Have you any other family?'

Alannah's vivid blue gaze rested for a thoughtful moment on the twisting hands of the older woman. 'No,' she said after a moment. 'Just Trina and me and my mother. My father died six months ago.'

The nervous hands stilled. 'I'm so sorry,' said the soft, pretty voice. 'Were you—I thought you said you'd been away for a year?'

'Yes. I went to a finishing school in Switzerland.' Alannah smiled selfconsciously. 'Mummy was so determined on it that I gave in. I was a year ahead at school anyway, so I haven't really missed anything. Daddy died while I was there.'

'You poor thing!' Mrs Hamel breathed sympathetically, forgetting her apprehension. 'So far from home . . .'

'Yes.' Alannah spoke quickly, for it still hurt. 'Of course I wanted to come home, but Rose—my mother—persuaded me that it would be silly to come back. And Daddy's sister in London came over to be with me and stayed two weeks. They were very kind to me at St. Antoine's.'

'Is that the aunt you stayed with in London?'

Alannah looked sideways at the mosaic of the Canterbury plains below, mostly in shades of brown and gold, and her heart beat high.

'Yes—Aunt Ria. She's a darling and gave me a super two months, but oh, I'm glad to be home! I've longed so for it.'

A note of excitement, of yearning too long suppressed, gave the clear young voice a strange maturity. Conscious of it, Alannah turned her head so that only her profile was visible, the flushed cheek hidden by a wave of dark red hair, thick and curly. Like silk, David had said once, smoothing a lock back from her forehead with his long fingers.

Her heart contracted, the rhythm of its beating accelerating in her ears. Perhaps David might be there to meet her too. Trina had said that he was very busy at the University at lectures as well as researching, but perhaps, if the fates were kind, today might be a slack day for him. It was over a year since they had seen each other, a long year without communication, and although darling Trina had done her best the news she enclosed in her letters hadn't satisfied Alannah's hungry heart.

Now, in a few minutes, perhaps she would see him, and her life would be complete again.

Even her profound grief at her father's missing figure could no more than dim her anticipation.

Mrs Hamel had been watching the delicate interplay of expression with shrewd, rather sad eyes. Now she said gently, 'Well, my dear, I hope everything turns out well for you. You—mercy!'

For as she spoke the plane went into the usual landing pandemonium, jets roaring with reverse thrust after the initial bounce as the wheels hit the runway.

'Well!' the older woman exclaimed. 'I didn't realise we were so close to landing. Thank you, honey.'

They said goodbye in the Customs Hall, then Alannah was in her mother's perfumed, silken embrace, and she and Trina and Rose wept together a little, remembering the fourth member of their family, gone now forever.

However, six months is long enough for the worst pangs of grief to have subsided, and although Alannah's heart jumped at the glimpse of a tall, fair man, she had realised almost immediately that David was not there. Hugging to herself the knowledge that very soon now she would see his dear face, she became infectiously gay, so that it was a brilliant, laughing trio who made their way home in two taxis, one for people, one for luggage.

'Blame Aunt Ria,' Alannah defended herself against Trina's teasing. 'She just can't resist beautiful clothes, and she was absurdly generous to me. I kept begging her to be sensible, but she only laughed and went on buying like a drunken sailor.'

'Lucky girl!' Trina grinned. 'I wonder if she'll do the same for me when I finally get to London.'

'Of course she will.' Alannah looked lovingly at her tall, beautiful sister. 'She'll be thrilled to have such a fabulous clothes-horse to dress. She kept saying rather wistfully that it was a pity I'm only five foot three.'

Their mother groaned. 'Not that old plaint, darling! You take after my side of the family, that's all. Plenty of men like little women, you know, it makes them feel protective.'

She viewed her unsatisfactory daughters with displeasure at their outrageous giggles, a displeasure which gradually relaxed into amusement. 'All right, but you wait and see! Now that you've lost a little weight, Alannah, you are just the right size for your height. You look—older, a little more sophisticated.'

'I should hope so!' Beneath the vivid blue scrutiny Rose had handed on to her elder daughter Alannah felt rather like an insect impaled on a pin, but St. Antoine's training held. She didn't wriggle, nor did she look selfconscious. 'My year away would have been an awfully expensive waste of time if I hadn't returned as polished as—as the dining room table!'

'Well, you were the most *un*polished schoolgirl I've had the misfortune to cope with.' Rose brooded gloomily on the younger Alannah, now, thank goodness, gone for ever, before brightening. 'I'm glad to see that that sullen, touch-me-not look you used to hide behind has gone, too. It was *so* off-putting, like having a changeling about the house!'

Alannah pushed back a brilliant lock of hair as she

wrinkled her nose at her mother. 'Never mind, Rose, you had a real charmer in Trina.'

Trina's deep voice was cross. 'Oh, lay off it, Allie!'

And their mother said seriously, 'Darling, you must get rid of this chip on your shoulder! There's no reason for you to be jealous of——'

'I'm *not* jealous of Trina!' Alannah smiled, but her voice and eyes were completely serious as she went on, 'I have never envied Trina, truly! How could I? She's a darling. Yes, you are, Trina, so don't look so disgusted! I know perfectly well that I'm obstinate and quick-tempered and far too quick to remember a grudge,' she grinned cheerfully at an oddly silent sister. 'How could I blame Trina for being nicer and sweeter than me? After all, Mama, she takes after you.'

Not at all averse to flattery, especially when so sincerely and lovingly offered, Rose Finderne said, 'Oh, *you!*' but there was the slightest hesitation in the soft, bright voice before she went on, 'Anyway, which of your new dresses are you going to wear to your party?'

'Party?'

'Darling, your birthday party! Or had you forgotten that you're almost nineteen?'

Alannah shook her head. 'No, no, of course not, but can we——?' She stopped, realising that the taxi driver could hear everything she was saying. 'Well, that's *super,*' she drawled, affecting an exaggerated Oxford accent that set Trina chuckling again.

But once in the elegant white house in the Cashmere Hills which had always been home, Alannah asked abruptly, 'Can we afford a party? I'd thought that with Dad—with Daddy gone, things might be a little difficult.'

Rose poured herself a second cup of tea, making the faint grimace which always accompanied any discussion of money. In her airiest tones she said, 'Darling, don't worry. Everything is under control, I promise you,' as Alannah's brows drew together.

'Are you sure?'

'Absolutely!' Rose was unexpectedly definite. 'There's nothing to stop you from having a marvellous time. Everyone knows you're home, and already there are invitations to more parties than I can count.'

'Not to mention David,' said Trina, her voice rather flat as her head turned. Through the window one could glimpse the gable of the house next door. Opie's house, where David lived.

Rose looked a little put out, but almost immediately her frown erased itself. Frowns cause wrinkles. 'Don't go putting ideas into Alannah's head,' she reproved. 'That was a boy and girl idyll, charming but quite insubstantial. David is a dear, but Alannah will probably find that they have very little in common now.'

But when at last they met again that evening it was not like that at all. They had not grown away from each other, as, deep in her subconscious, Alannah had feared. Instead she flew into his arms and his beloved blond head bent at the dazzled invitation of her mouth and eyes as they exchanged their first adult kiss apart from the last starved, desperate embrace before she had left for Switzerland.

'Darling,' he whispered at last, his normally level voice slightly roughened with emotion. 'Darling, oh, Alannah, I've missed you so!'

Fiercely she nuzzled his throat, burying her face in the warmth. 'I'm so glad to be back,' she said tightly. 'It's been purgatory.'

'Yes.'

That was all, that was all that needed to be said.

Growing up together as they had, David only three years older than her, there had always been an affinity between them, until when she was sixteen Alannah had realised that their friendship and affection had been transformed into something else. For a few months she had anguished over the loss of their happy comradeship, until David kissed her. Gently, that first time, as if he was afraid of frightening her, but her candid, generous response had taken him by surprise and he had withdrawn a little, become serious and adult as he had explained that for both of them it would be better not to allow themselves to be lured into too close a relationship.

Both of them led busy fulfilled lives, he at university, she still at school, so it had not been too difficult to remain loving friends. Until Rose's decision to send her to finishing school had forced them into each other's arms, and then it was only David's strength of will which had prevented exactly the thing Rose feared.

So they had had their testing time, their year apart, and now, surely even Rose could see that they were meant for each other.

Although in the days that followed Rose made no open protest her attitude caused Alannah a deep-seated unease. All attempts to ask her why she objected to their relationship were evaded; in the end Alannah attributed her mother's muted displeasure to the fact that Rose disapproved of early marriages. She could—and did—quote any number of people whose relationships had come unstuck because they were too young for the responsibility.

So Alannah, who had no intention of marrying for at least a year, not until David had got his Doctorate, gave up her attempts to pin Rose down and settled to the exquisite pleasure of re-learning all that there was to know about him, in between going to parties, enrolling at university and thoroughly enjoying herself.

Just before the first guest arrived at her nineteenth

birthday party a rapturously happy girl made her graceful way down the splendid staircase, her face lit from within by anticipation.

'Darling, you look superb,' Rose said fondly. 'I do wish Daddy was here to see you.'

Mother and daughter touched hands, the same pensive proud expression touching each face. Although the first access of grief was past Holt Finderne was very much missed by his family.

'Perhaps he can,' Alannah said quietly, only just stifling a nervous giggle.

Rose sighed. 'I had hoped that a year in St. Antoine's would have got rid of that wretched giggle of yours.'

'Most of the time I can control it,' her daughter said, a little defensively. 'And they worked very hard on it! Remember how it used to pop out at the most inopportune moments?'

'Oh, I do indeed.' Rose made a little moue before running a slender, diamonded finger across her brow. 'Only too well, I'm afraid. If there was ever a moment when a giggle could make things worse there was that infernal giggle. I remember your father trying rather desperately to remember that it was an involuntary reaction to stress after it had made him so mad he wanted to smack you severely. Infinite embarrassment you were, to yourself and to us! If that's all St. Antoine's did for you it was worth it.'

Alannah pirouetted across the wide hall, slender and insubstantial in floating pink chiffon which should have clashed badly with the glowing, vivid mass of her hair. That it didn't was the result of Rose's fashion cunning.

'I may not be very good at painting,' she was prone to saying, 'but I can blend colours in clothes.'

It was true, as even her most envious friends agreed. Now, viewing her daughter with an eye in which the maternal and artistic were nicely entwined, she nodded with quiet satisfaction as Alannah said:

'Aha, but that isn't all! Behold me, ready to run a house with skill and panache. I even know how to hire and fire servants! So useful here in New Zealand where servants are remarkably thin on the ground. Still, as well as order a meal I can cook one, and I know exactly what to say to any important men my future husband must pander to.'

'Oh, don't sound so—so cynical!' Rose snapped in a manner most unlike her usual composed self. 'As well as that sort of thing— and there's no need to sneer, I still feel that a woman's most important function is to be as good a wife and mother as she can—you've acquired an appreciation of art, and music and other cultural things that will give you pleasure all of your life.'

Remorsefully Alannah slipped an arm through her mother's, careful not to crush the elegant muted silk of her dress. She had her own ideas where her appreciation of art and music came from, remembering happy times spent listening to and discussing such things with her father, but because Rose seemed a little on edge she didn't pursue the matter, although she did say peaceably:

'Well, now I want to go to university and become as knowledgeable about computers.'

From the stairs came the dry voice of her sister, 'And eventually become Mrs David Opie.'

Hardly the most tactful of times to introduce the subject. Wildfire colour touched Alannah's fine pale skin. 'That,' she responded carefully, 'is not on the cards just yet.'

'Darling, you're *far* too young—both of you! I was talking to Renee Opie only a few days ago and she said that David has great plans for the future,' Rose said quickly, dabbing fretfully at a non-existent crease in her dress. She moved away from Alannah and pushed back a lock of Trina's hair, continuing a little loudly, 'If you were thinking of marrying an older man it might be different. Maturity is so important in marriage. Much as I love David, one must admit that he's only a boy yet. You young things have so many options, so much to take advantage of, and yet so many of you tie yourselves down far too early. Trina, how lovely you look! How lovely you both look! Shall we make a quick final tour?'

The sisters exchanged glances, Alannah's slightly reproachful one met with a kind of cool blandness from Trina, and a cold foreboding feathered along her skin. For a moment she hesitated, but Rose, her gaiety restored, was holding out a hand to each and with a swift mental shrug she joined her mother and sister.

Caught up in Rose's blithe spirits, she managed to forget her apprehension. Together they toured the house, admiring her mother's positive brilliance when it came to setting the scene for pleasure.

'It may be a frivolous talent,' Rose observed with some complacence after Trina's praise, 'but it's my own. I seem to know instinctively what will please people.'

She looked both her daughters over with a cool critical regard which softened when no fault could be found with either of them. They smiled back, well used to this quick, sharp summing up. Rose had incredibly high standards and from childhood they had been assessed like this. They made a superb contrast. Alannah was half a head shorter than her more statuesque sister, delicate with mobile features, and her rich cloud of hair emphasised by her only other claims to beauty, her great blue eyes and wilful, ardent mouth. Trina's hair was chestnut, more restrained than her sister's riotous curls, and she was a classic beauty like her mother with eyes of a strange colour between green and gold. Tonight, because she wore a dress of gold, they were also gold, lit by a glitter of excitement, which was unusual, as she was the serene one of the two.

As she gazed around at the flower-filled sitting room, mellow and gracious with antiques and Persian rugs, and the crisp contrast of white walls and ceilings, Alannah felt her heart swell. The year away had been fascinating, but homesickness had made it never-ending, and when Holt Finderne had died she had wept into the telephone, begging to be allowed to come home.

Half the world away Rose too had wept, but she had been adamant. So Alannah had lived out her year in exile and now she was being rewarded for her obedience. Home at last, this time for good, with her friends due at any minute. And David.

Only her father's absence darkened the brilliance of her gaze, but as she was young and very much in love, she managed to ignore that silent grief.

And soon there was music and laughter and David's hand around hers. Like a Christmas fairy she sparkled, vivacious and glittering, her laughter unforced and free from shadow.

Later, taking a few rapturous minutes off from her duties as hostess, she danced, lost in David's arms, her expression softly absorbed.

'I've missed you so,' he whispered, tightening his hold fractionally.

'Mmm.' She was happy, so happy that she thought if she died at this moment she would die fulfilled.

'Is that all you can say?' David sounded indignant, but she had known him so long that she wasn't fooled.

'What do you want me to say?' she asked, slanting a flirtatious look up through her lashes.

A hard colour patched his cheekbones. 'Don't,' he groaned, suddenly easing his grip. 'If I told you you'd probably die of shock and horror! This year's been endless! I know your mother's reasoning was sound when she asked us not to write as a kind of test, but oh, my darling, it's been hell!'

Alannah stirred, awed by the intensity of his tone. Unconsciously trying to lighten the situation, she said, 'I know, David. But I'm sure you've been too busy to pine. Trina has kept me posted about how hard you've been working.'

'You were always there,' he said, controlled once more, smiling tenderly down at her. 'All the time. Everything I've done I did for you—for us.'

It was the nearest he had ever come to proposing. Solemn, so happy that she was choked by it, Alannah lifted her eyes to his. They exchanged a long, brilliant look, their eyes saying much which as yet had not been spoken between them. Then David's glance shifted, and his expression changed.

'What is it?' she asked.

He hesitated before saying slowly. 'Someone's just come in. He was staring rather obviously at us, but he's stopped now. He's talking to your mother.'

'Who is it?'

David frowned. 'I don't know, yet the face seems familiar.' He swung her around. 'There, you can see him now.'

It took only one glance for Alannah to recognise him, Never, not these last three years, not if she lived to be ninety, would she forget that cold, handsome countenance, dark-skinned, set with eyes of such piercing icy green that the memory of them still froze her. She drew a ragged breath, missing the step, and turned a white face away from the man who was now greeting her mother.

'Darling who is it? Alannah——?'

'Nicholas Challoner.'

'Nicholas——' He stopped abruptly. 'Challoner?'

The one——?'

'Yes. The Nicholas Challoner whose wife I killed on my sixteenth birthday.'

He was silent, his feet moving automatically to the music flowing past them. Shivering, rigid with shock, Alannah felt completely alone, detached even from the warmth of David's embrace, lost in a cold, forgotten prison where the only reality was the icy condemnation of Nicholas Challoner's eyes.

'What the hell is he doing here?' David's outraged voice sounded thin and far away. 'Did your mother invite him, or was it his own idea to turn up like a bloody ghost at the banquet?'

She had to answer him. Speaking slowly, through lips suddenly numb, she said, 'Rose said nothing about him coming.'

'She doesn't seem surprised to see him.' David's glance was suddenly sharp. 'Come on, we're going to have something to drink. And it won't be the lemonade you've been sipping all evening, either. You've had a shock and you need something stronger.'

He gave her a small amount of brandy and took her out on to the terrace to drink it, standing beside her as she sipped it, his glance bent broodingly on the panorama of Christchurch spread out below them, all lights and glitter like a fairy city on its plain between the mountains and the sea.

'Don't let his presence intimidate you,' he said softly. 'What happened was a complete accident.'

'If I hadn't lost control of my skateboard and shot out in front of her she wouldn't have gone over the bank,' Alannah said in the toneless voice of one repeating a lesson learned by rote.

'The inquest proved that it wasn't your fault,' he insisted. 'Just one of those hideous happenings, a complete accident with faults on both sides. I thought you were over it! What the hell is Rose up to?'

Alannah shivered. 'She was six months pregnant. She died and so did the baby. I went—I went with Daddy to tell him how sorry I was, and he—he hated me.'

'He was in shock. He'll be over that now.'

He spoke soothingly, but she barely heard his voice, lost in the memories she had fought so hard to repress. 'His face was like a mask, all except his eyes. They were icy-cold, so cold they burnt me. I—I wanted to say how sorry I was for what I'd done, but I could only—it was Daddy who told him. Daddy held my hand all the time. Nicholas Challoner said almost nothing, but his eyes looked at me as if I was beneath contempt. I was so nervous I couldn't stop giggling when we'd got outside that horrible hotel room. I was almost beside myself.'

David held her close, his face in her hair. 'Darling, *don't*! He's probably just come to—to say he's sorry, or over it, or something.'

His clumsy attempt at comfort failed. 'Did he look as if he was over it?' she demanded unevenly. 'He was like a statue, cold and shiny and beautiful and cruel. He's still like that.'

David sighed, holding her away from him so that he could give her a little shake. 'Now you're getting hysterical. Stop it, Alannah! He can't hurt you. It was a shattering experience and because you're a sensitive little thing it's left an indelible mark on you, but you mustn't allow it to overshadow your life. What happened was a cruel stroke of fate; neither you nor Mrs Challoner were entirely to blame. The truck roaring up the hill stopped you from hearing her and the bush made it impossible for her to see you. She acted entirely instinctively in avoiding you, and it was sheer bad luck that killed her. As you must remember, the police decided that she must have revved a bit hard to get up the hill and was going too fast. Now, are you going to pull yourself together, or do I have to send you to bed?'

Shuddering, recalled to the present by the hard note in his voice, Alannah made an immense effort to regain control. 'I'm O.K.,' she said after a few moments.

'That's my girl!' He dropped a kiss on her mouth, light, comforting.

Alannah's hands clenched on his arms; she swayed, seeking more, seeking reassurance that he would protect her.

He hesitated, then, mistaking her plea, bent his head to meet her mouth, his own openly sensuous. For the first time Alannah missed the singing delight his touch normally aroused. Nicholas Challoner's sudden appearance had robbed her of that warmth of response. David's kiss was sweet, but within her she was frozen and he didn't know it.

Some instinct made her pull away. David murmured her name just as another voice, deeper, harshly controlled, overrode it.

'I'm sorry to break up this charming idyll, Alannah, but your mother wants you with her. Something to do with a birthday cake, I believe.'

For a moment Alannah stood stock still, every process of her body suspended. Then she turned and said politely to Nicholas Challoner, 'Very well.'

Somehow she moved, somehow found herself back in that laughing, crowded room, David just a little behind, her whole being absorbed in the man who walked with lithe animal grace beside her. Rose was smiling, her expression so normal that insensibly Alannah relaxed. But while she cut her birthday cake and laughed and thanked her guests for their good wishes, while the usual cheerful pandemonium went on, that dark presence was like a brooding shadow over her.

And afterwards, when supper had been eaten and the band struck up again, it was with a sigh of something like relief that she went into his arms. At last she would know what he was doing here.

He held her loosely in the conventional manner, but she fancied that his touch was a manacle, shackling her to him. Cold dismay crawled across her skin. He was tall, about six feet, and his shoulders were wide with the kind of strength she could feel through the material of his jacket. Long-legged, narrow-hipped, with hands which were thin and well-shaped, he had a superb physical presence only slightly enhanced by features of angular masculine beauty.

Alannah met the envious stare of an old friend and forced herself to smile back. Before supper the music had been disco-style, but the band had changed now to romantic ballads. Most of the dancers were swaying together, using the dance as an excuse to get closer to each other. Across the room David was talking to Trina; he seemed absorbed in what he was saying, but as she watched he glanced up and gave her an encouraging smile. He was a million miles away. Nicholas Challoner had the power to wall her away from the world like a Vestal Virgin found to be virgin no longer.

When he spoke she tensed, every muscle in her body taut for a second.

'Three years has made quite a difference,' he said, the cruel deliberation of his words driving the colour from her face.

'Is that why you came? To see what I'd grown into?' She didn't want to look at him, she kept her eyes fixed on his shoulder until at last his will dragged her glance upward.

To meet eyes filled with cold amusement.

'Partly,' he said, scanning her face with insolent thoroughness. 'But mainly because Rose invited me.'

If he had hit her she would have been less astounded. '*Rose?* But why——?'

The unfinished question hovered between them. For a moment she thought he was not going to answer it, until she felt the muscles of his shoulder move in an infinitesimal shrug, and he drawled, 'Why not? Rose and I have become quite friendly during the past few months. And before that I saw your father frequently.'

When she could not hide her astonishment he smiled with great unkindness. 'Didn't they tell you, Alannah?' Well, that might be because I ordered them not to.'

'*Ordered?*' The one word came roughly from a throat almost raw with tension.

'Did I say ordered? Obviously that was a mistake.'

But it hadn't been. Alannah's wide, frightened eyes were fixed on the harsh handsome face; something she saw there set the muscles quivering in her throat as she tried to swallow. Instantly his eyes fell to the smooth pale column. She crimsoned at the hunger she saw reflected in that roving sensual gaze and for the first time wished that she had worn a dress which didn't reveal so much. Compared to some in the room it was modest, but Nicholas Challoner looked at her as if she had stripped for his pleasure.

'Did you enjoy your year away?'

The question helped her regain some sort of composure. Dragging her eyes away, she said, 'Yes. It—it was fun. Interesting, too.'

'I believe your sister has decided against a similar year. She's taking an expensive course, medicine. Your mother will have to subsidise her fairly heavily.'

Once more her eyes flew to meet his in painful question, once more they met cold mockery.

'Yes,' she said, striving for some sort of dignity. He was playing a game, one to which she didn't know the rules. Help me, her heart screamed as she looked over his shoulder, but David was dancing with Trina and her mother was talking with great animation to two of her dearest friends.

'She has a real sense of mission, so Rose tells me.'

'Yes.'

The deep, smooth voice became lower, more intimate. 'And what do you plan to do, now that you're home?'

Anger spurted up within her. 'Don't you know?' she asked sweetly, smiling at her mother, whose answering smile almost hid the wary question in the sharp, stabbing glance she sent across the room.

'Well, yes, as it happens, I do,' he said, answering her false smile with a movement of his own lips, as empty of emotion. He lowered his head and continued softly, 'But I doubt if you do, Alannah.'

There was no doubt about the cold triumph, the purposeful implacability of that last sentence. Alannah's body jerked in rejection; instantly his hands tightened on her.

Then the music stopped and he walked her across to where Rose waited, and surely she could not be the only one in the room to see the pitiless lack of mercy beneath the charming surface?

Apparently she was. Rose was her usual laughing self, spreading a cloak of gaiety over the situation so that after a few tense moments Alannah found herself responding. Trina and David joined them and Alannah had to watch, hiding her agony, as Nicholas Challoner masterfully charmed them both into instant liking. It seemed that only she could see the total possession in his glance whenever it rested on her.

'You see,' said David later as they danced once more, 'he's obviously forgiven and forgotten. From something Rose said I gather he had business dealings with your father. They must have become friendly but decided not to tell you in case you were upset.'

It sounded logical. Only Alannah knew that it was not as simple as that. 'I'm afraid,' she said beneath her breath, but David's reaction was one of barely concealed impatience.

'You're being silly, darling. He's an incredibly charismatic guy. In fact, if you weren't so silly, I'd be jealous. Men like that tend to cause havoc in feminine breasts!'

He was joking and she responded, but it was a much diminished imitation of her usual brilliant smile.

'Rose should have told you,' David decided now. 'It was cruel to spring him on you like that. Still, it's over. You can start the rest of your life without his shadow hanging over you.'

How could he be so obtuse? She felt like screaming at him, striking at his pleasantly regular features, anything to force him to realise what was happening under his eyes. Nicholas Challoner was not a shadow, he was very real, very much in the flesh, and he was looming over her, shutting out the light, cutting her off from the rest of humanity.

If anyone had asked her she would have said that she and David were perfectly attuned, their minds and hearts linked in a bond which time and love had forged, which was unbreakable. But as she looked up into his face, her own unconsciously pleading, she trembled with the realisation that he was completely won over by Nicholas Challoner's outward persona, that mask he assumed to hide the ruthless man beneath. She was alone, as she had never been before, not even when she suffered from the knowledge that she had caused Ngaire Challoner's death. Then her parents had understood and comforted her, helping her to accept herself, coaxing her out of her anguish. Oh, Daddy, she cried silently, but there was no longer a Daddy to protect her. This unknown threat was one she would have to face alone and unarmed.

'Sweetheart, you look exhausted,' David told her tenderly. 'I think jet-lag must have finally caught up with you, poor little love. Make sure you sleep in tomorrow.'

'I'll do that.' Was that her voice, toneless, all life gone from it?

It was three in the morning before the party broke up, and when, after locking up the house, Alannah went in search of her mother it was to find Trina closing the door of the big bedroom behind her. When she saw her sister she shook her head, putting her finger to her lips.

'Headache,' she whispered.

Alannah nodded wearily. Rose always ended a party with a tension headache. Tomorrow morning would see it gone and her mother brighter than anyone else in the house. Until then it would be impossible to demand an explanation of Nicholas Challoner's appearance.

After a whispered goodnight she went into her bedroom, took off her clothes and her make-up, then fell into bed and slept as if poleaxed.

CHAPTER TWO

Sure enough, next morning Rose was her usual cheerful self, answering Alannah's questions with patient frankness.

'Well, as soon as I saw you I realised I should have told you he was coming, but at the time it seemed the sensible decision to make, darling. I thought you might be nervous and that it would spoil the party for you.'

Alannah pushed at her brow, trying to knead away a tightness across her forehead. 'But why did you invite him? How well do you know him?'

'Oh, quite well.' Her mother sipped coffee. 'We never lost touch after the accident. And he has interests in the same areas as your father. He's been very good to me since Holt died.'

There was an odd silence. Rose's tapered forefinger with its perfect rosy nail traced the pattern on the china, a stylised flower as delicate as Rose herself.

'How good?' Alannah's question made a harsh counterpoint to the warm golden morning.

'Very good.' Rose looked at her but quickly lowered her lashes. 'I know he seems a little—hard, but he's really very kind.'

'Kind?' Alannah thought of the three dances she had been forced to endure in his arms, the contemptuous ease with which he had made banal conversation after the first one, and couldn't prevent the note of incredulity in her voice. '*Kind?*'

'Yes, kind,' her mother said firmly, setting her coffee cup back on its saucer. 'Now, let's get things tidy, shall we? The house smells like a bar!'

It didn't, of course. The firm of caterers who had made such a perfect job of the supper had left the place immaculate, but, intensely fastidious, Rose was not satisfied until well after lunch that everything was as it should be. Then Trina went off to spend the rest of the afternoon with a friend and Rose had a rest, leaving Alannah, restless and still strung up, to walk in the garden, wishing fervently that David had not had to meet a visiting dignitary with his professor.

The day was sunwarmed and clear, and inevitably, in its light her fears of last night seemed like the fantasies of an overheated brain. Of course Nicholas Challoner posed no threat to her! It was impossible that they could ever be friends, but she must indeed have been suffering from jet-lag to imagine that they were deadly enemies.

She had just reached this comforting conclusion when she stopped, appalled to find that her steps had led her to the exact spot where she had hurtled in front of Ngaire Challoner that day three years ago. The enormous rhododendron which has hidden her so successfully was still there. Blindly she stepped out on to the roadway, then screamed, leaping back into the branches as a big car came to a halt within inches of her trembling form.

He was swearing as he flung open the door, swearing as he shook her by the upper arms until she sagged, her hands holding back more screams.

'Trying it a second time?' he demanded savagely. 'Bad luck, Alannah, I'm not tender-hearted enough to drive over the bank to save a stupid adolescent! Stop that bloody noise!'

For a moment she thought she was going to faint. The world receded into blackness and there was a dreadful humming in her ears. Another imprecation made her shake with terror, then strong arms lifted her and she was thrust into the car. Eyes tight shut, trying to stop the rigours which shook her body, a scream held back only by an effort of will so strong she could concentrate on nothing else, she lay back in the seat while the car wound up the hill to come to rest beneath the wide *porte-cochère* over the front door.

'Get out,' he commanded, and she did, her usual spirited independence lost in the shock of his appearance.

He didn't take her inside; strong fingers marked her skin as he urged her towards a small summerhouse.

By the time they reached it Alannah had recovered some shreds of poise. She jerked her arm in an attempt to pull away. But those fingers tightened cruelly before he forced her down on to the narrow bench-seat around the wall.

Incongruously outlined against a brilliant waterfall of pink roses, he looked her over, taking in her obvious effort to regain her self-possession and the enormous bruised eyes which revealed how fragile it was.

'Are you determined to commit suicide at that particular spot?' he asked brutally.

Alannah winced, turning her face away from a scrutiny which was totally lacking in emotion. 'Oh God, you gave me such a fright!' she gasped huskily.

'I can see that. Where's your mother?'

'Resting.'

Those frigid green eyes swept her face. 'So should you be, by the look of you. Did your boy-friend keep you up too late?'

Defiance lit small fires at the back of her eyes. 'That's none of your business,' she retorted slowly, daring him to say more.

His smile was hateful. 'No? Well, perhaps you're right. Tell me, Alannah Finderne, how fond are you of your mother?'

Sheer astonishment robbed her of speech. Her mouth fell a little open as she stared at him. 'What?'

'You heard. At our first meeting—which I'm sure you remember—I gathered the impression that you were Daddy's girl. However, after seeing you last night, I'm wondering if perhaps that first impression wasn't too simplistic. You do love your mother, I suppose?'

Alannah swallowed, completely at a loss to understand him. Last night's fear had returned in all its darkness. Speaking almost randomly she said, 'Of course. I mean—of *course* I love her!'

'Oh, there's no "of course" about it,' he told her with such profound cynicism in his voice that she flinched. 'Filial love is not an altogether common commodity. And Trina? Just how do you feel about her? A certain amount of sibling rivalry is to be expected; she is, after all, better looking than you even now and shows every sign of being a beauty when she grows up. Envious? Jealous?'

'You're mad!' Alannah spoke with such complete conviction that he began to laugh softly, with real amusement.

'No,' he said, putting out a hand to stop her as she jumped to her feet. The long fingers closed around the slender, deceptively fragile bones of her wrist with sensuous enjoyment, tightening until the pain brought her up short, gasping, her blue eyes wild as they fixed with painful intensity on his dark face.

Incredulously she realised that her pain gave him pleasure; her jaw tightened and she stopped struggling.

The amusement died in his face. One lean finger tipped her chin and he stared at the still, proud curve of her mouth. When his glance flicked up to meet her eyes she saw a heat in the hard green depths which made her draw in her breath painfully.

'No,' he said again, almost as though reminding

himself of something. 'Tell me, Alannah, what would you do for your mother and your sister?'

'Why do you want to know?'

He let her wrist go, sliding his hand up her arm. Beneath its strength her skin prickled and a curious lassitude rendered her limbs heavy. Twisting free, she stepped back and sat down again, refusing to glance his way, but so conscious of him that she could feel his nearness in her very bones.

'Your mother told me you were surprised that she was able to give you such a large party,' he said, the smooth toneless voice frightening on the warm scented air.

In spite of her resolution not to look his way again this unwelcome intimation of an unwelcome intimacy between him and Rose sent her eyes darting upwards.

She met an enigmatic gaze and asked harshly, 'Why should that interest you? What do you want, Mr Challoner? Why are you tormenting me like this?'

'Tormenting?'

Just one word, yet it held a world of taunting implication; his voice made his contempt for her youth and emotional condition so clear that all colour fled her skin. Her eyes dropped to where her hands lay in taut stillness in her lap.

A late bee struggled from the centre of a rose, its legs and abdomen yellow with pollen. It blundered around for a short time before orienting itself to some distant hive, then flew off in a straight, sure line. Below them a car horn sounded stridently. There was a burst of laughter and the sound of an engine being started. Somewhere someone was using a power mower to cut a lawn, far enough away for the sound to be a pleasant hum. The sun beat down and in the little summerhouse the air was heavy and scented, but Alannah shivered, her skin tightening against a threat which was coming ever closer.

She refused to speak again, waiting for Nicholas Challoner to initiate any further conversation. After some minutes he did so, his voice as deliberate and correct as if he was discussing the weather.

'I'm curious about you,' he said. 'I came to see if the sullen adolescent I remembered had altered in any important way.'

'And?'

'Oh, not very much. The years, ably helped by your finishing school, have changed you from a schoolgirl to a desirable young woman. You appear to have a little more to say for yourself. And you still lie in wait for unwary drivers.'

Goaded, Alannah sprang to her feet, a hand upraised. He said nothing, but there was that in his face which brought her, shaken and intimidated, to her senses.

Then Rose called from the house. Alannah flew up the hill towards her as if she was an angel of deliverance. Indeed, to Alannah's overwrought imagination, she seemed just that. Rose sent her daughter to make afternoon tea; shortly after that Nicholas Challoner drove away, and not so very much later David came over.

In Rose's presence they didn't kiss, but he took Alannah's hand, squeezing it so hard that she flinched.

'Sorry,' he said, laughing, his pale eyes alight with excitement. 'I didn't mean to hurt you, but I've just had the most incredibly good news!'

'What?' Alannah was infected by his excitement, warming herself in his presence.

'Well, this V.I.P. I had to escort around has a scholarship in his belt! Apparently he's been asked to recommend a man for a position in America, and after Dr James had talked to him he's decided on me!'

'But that's marvellous!' Alannah hugged him. 'How clever you are! Where do you go?'

'Oh, Los Angeles. I do a stint at university there, but most of my time is spent with one of the foremost labs in my kind of work!'

Alannah was thrilled for him, but a chill of premonition brushed across her emotions. Ignoring it, she asked, 'How long will you be away?'

'Two years.' For a moment his excitement faded as he looked into her carefully composed face. 'Alannah——' he began, but was interrupted by Rose's brisk voice.

'Two years nothing,' she said, and smiled. 'Dear David, you deserve your scholarship; you've worked like a slave ever since we've known you.'

In her steady gaze there was a warning. Although Alannah felt an intense blind rebellion welling up she knew that her mother was right. She must say and do nothing to spoil his delight at this unexpected luck. No, she told herself fiercely, this was not luck. This he deserved! And, as he had waited a year for her, uncomplaining and faithful, she would do the same for him. Her glance glowed with pride as it rested on his face. He was talking eagerly, telling them both of the advantages of such a period in America, his bluntly handsome features irradiated by excitement.

A wave of love overcame her. Careless of her mother's presence, she kissed his cheek. His hand came up and he pulled her closer to him as he continued talking.

Trina arrived back, was told the news and burst into tears, so startling them all that only David had the presence of mind to hold her and console her gently.

'I'm such a f-*fool*!' she sobbed, wiping her eyes with the handkerchief he gave her. 'It's just that I—that things are finishing. First Alannah went away and when she came back I thought everything was g-going to be like it used to be, and now David's going, and nothing w-will ever be the same!'

She gulped and was patted and hugged by them all, and while David and Rose went off to get one of the bottles of champagne left over from the night before, Alannah comforted her.

'Oh, don't take any notice of me,' Trina said trenchantly, sniffing. 'Too much sympathy and I'll bawl again. How can you be so calm when you know you won't see him for two years?'

'It hasn't really sunk in yet,' Alannah told her honestly, adding with a wintry smile. 'Just don't be surprised if you hear great sobs halfway through the night!'

Trina gulped, and said, 'Oh, I do love you, Ally,' and hugged her severely as Rose and David came back, bearing the champagne in triumph.

He left a week later, promising to write but without making any effort to formalise their still unspoken agreement. Alannah waved the great jet off with a pale, tearless face, before allowing herself to be swept off by his parents and Rose to lunch at a city restaurant.

If her laughter was forced it went unremarked. David's mother, too, had a suspicious brightness in her eyes and a strained note in her voice.

It was during the meal that Alannah realised that someone was watching her from across the room. At first she did not recognise him, but when he lifted his glass in mocking acknowledgment she felt the colour drain from her face. What was Nicholas Challoner doing here? His base was Auckland in the North Island. What could have kept him here in Christchurch for so long?

As the questions buzzed through her brain she forced herself to eat, to reply to the remarks addressed to her. With only partial success, for she knew immediately when he rose and could feel her skin prickle at every step he took across the room towards them.

Rose noticed him first and greeted him warmly. 'Nick, my dear! You've met Mr and Mrs Opie, of course, David's parents. We've just waved him off to America.'

He was polite, very charming; the Opies were impressed. Alannah sat very still, toying with her coffee cup, as if she could make herself completely inconspicuous. But eventually those green eyes came to rest on her small, remote face.

'You look depressed, Alannah,' he said smoothly. 'Would you like to come with me this afternoon? I'm going to drive down to see some friends.'

'An excellent idea!' Rose was definite, her expression firmly sympathetic. 'Darling, go with Nick. If you don't you'll mope for the rest of the day.'

Alannah lifted her lashes. Slowly, inexorably, she was being manipulated. Instinct told her that it was no use looking to her mother for rescue.

'Very well,' she said in a small, colourless voice.

Nicholas's friends were pleasant, a couple with an almost vertical sheep farm on Bank's Peninsula, that large protrusion formed aeons ago by volcanoes which makes such an immense contrast to the sweeping plains between it and the Southern Alps. Normally Alannah would have enjoyed their company. They were obviously fond of Nick Challoner, but somewhat in awe of him, and when he introduced her both recognised her name, although neither made any comment.

They stayed for two hours. When they left he drove straight home and came in with her.

'Rose isn't here,' she said quietly.

'I know.' He met her quick glance with a cool smile. 'She mentioned a fashion parade. Are you not interested in fashion, Alannah?'

'Not today.'

'You'd rather mope for the boy-friend?'

She bit her lip as she led the way into the drawing room. 'Won't you sit down? Can I get you something to drink?'

'So soon after that incredible afternoon tea?' He waited until she had sat down before taking a chair directly opposite so that he could see her, small and untouched in the elegant French armchair, her hair glowing like an aureole about her tense face.

'What do you want?' she asked stubbornly.

'You,' he said.

Surprisingly the softly-delivered monosyllable did not astonish her, but her nails clenched painfully on to the soft palms of her hands.

'Exactly how?' she asked remotely.

'As my wife.'

This time her eyes flew to his face. It had not altered, not changed in expression at all, the hard, handsome lines seemingly carved from granite. Involuntarily Alannah shivered.

'To take the place of the one I killed?'

'That exactly.' And when she said nothing in answer he continued, 'And to supply me with the child you killed, too.'

Very carefully she unclenched her fingers. Where they had met her palms there were pale half-moons; as she watched they filled in and became red. It seemed very important to keep her eyes on them. Perhaps if she looked at them long enough he would go away and she could forget the wrenching terror which had her in thrall.

On the mantel a clock ticked peaceably, a sound from her childhood. It was stupid to be so afraid that her brain refused to function. Of course he could not force her to marry him.

She said so.

A long silent moment passed before he answered, 'Of course I can, Alannah. Do you really think I expected you to agree? Even if I had, one glance at you with your besotted gaze on David Opie's face and I'd have known better. I don't believe in failure.'

'You sent him away.'

He nodded, heavy lids half-closed as he watched her. 'I wondered how long it would take you to work that out.'

Terror gripped her by the throat. One slender hand came up to touch it as though she could clear the obstruction from the exterior. 'And my mother?'

'Rose?' He smiled, not a pleasant smile. 'By the time your father died his investments were in a dangerous state. Your mother was only too grateful for advice—and help. If that help was to be withdrawn . . .' He said no more, but he did not need to.

'Why?' When he made no answer she whispered, 'Why me? I came—I came to tell you that I was sorry. It was an accident——'

'And I would have accepted your apology, sullen though it was, if I hadn't heard you laugh as soon as you got outside the door.'

The note of savage anger in the harsh voice brought her head up, but he was on his feet, moving with the swiftness of a striking beast. Before Alannah had a chance to defend herself his hand was wrapped in the hair at the nape of her head, pulling her head back to expose her face and the tender arc of her throat to his gaze.

'I was nervous,' she said huskily, dampening lips dry with fear. 'I used to—to giggle——'

'Shut up!' His fingers tightened viciously in the soft tendrils, causing tears to drown her eyes. 'I loved my wife,' he said, white around the mouth. 'And you killed her and our child. You owe me, Alannah, and for once in your life you're going to pay. It shouldn't be too hard. I don't want love or affection or companionship. I don't want anything from you but the use of your body, and that I will have.'

As if the touch of her contaminated him he dragged his hand free from the living silk of her hair, brushing it with his other while a muscle flicked against his jaw. A hard flush lay along his cheekbones. He looked at her as if she was the lowliest creature on God's earth, his contempt icing over the anger.

But Alannah was on her feet too, her fear lost for the moment in a torrent of fury. 'You arrogant swine!' she spat 'Find some other brood mare to carry your children for you! I'm damned if I'm going to! It's *obscene*.'

'Perhaps.' He appeared to be once more in command of himself, for the word was drawled and his breathing slowed, resuming its even pace. 'Obscenity is in the eye of the beholder. I find you bed-worthy, Alannah, and I don't care whether or not you enjoy the conception of my children. You'll conceive as often as I want you to. As for being damned—well, you'll certainly be damned if you don't. Not only you, my dear, but pretty, silly Rose, and Trina. Not to mention the boy-friend.'

She had turned her back on him while she strove for some measure of self-control, but this last sentence, delivered in a voice that was a threat in itself, made her swing around, her expression distraught as she took in the implication.

'What—what do you mean?'

'The whole idea of the scholarship was to get him out of the way. If he's not, then I can see no reason why my money should provide him with exactly what he wants.'

'He wants me,' she said fiercely, taking a step towards him in her anger.

'He wants this scholarship more. Why didn't he marry you and take you with him?'

She flew at him, fingers hooked, striking for his eyes. Blood rushed to her head; as he caught her she struggled with primitive ferocity, once catching him on the face with a nail. His hands were ruthless, enforcing a bitter subjection, shaking her until she went limp, her tormented eyes fixed on his face.

'I'll never forgive you,' she whispered as if she made a solemn vow. '*Never*, not until the day I die.'

He showed his teeth at that. 'Never is a long day, you little hellcat.' A sound made him turn his head. 'That must be Rose. A remarkable woman, your mother—invariably punctual. I hope you have the same qualities.'

She flushed in naked, painful awareness of the taunt in his voice and words. He was telling her that he despised Rose as much as he hated her daughter, that both of them deserved the worst life could hand them.

'If I don't marry you, what will you do?' she whispered as her mother's car came to a halt in the garage.

'Reduce you all to poverty. No medical school for Trina, it will be straight to work in whatever job she can get. Everything will go to pay debts.' His cold glance swept around the lovely room with its collection of much-loved antiques. 'There won't be enough money to buy you a house, however small in the worst part of town. I doubt if even in her youth Rose could have managed love in a cottage; she's less likely to cope now. She has always been an expensive lady.'

As Rose's light footsteps sounded along the passage her daughter said lifelessly, 'Very well, then. You hold all the cards.'

'Of course.' He smiled at the bitter anguish in her expression and took her by the shoulders, pulling her inexorably against him. 'Then let's seal our bargain in the usual way, shall we?'

So that when Rose entered the room it was to see them locked together, Nicholas's mouth sealing her daughter's closed, his arms holding the small, straight form pressed hard against him. If she noticed that Alannah showed no signs of responding she said nothing about it then, or later.

That afternoon something died within Alannah, everything warm and tender, leaving only the cold shell of a person.

When Nicholas had gone she followed her mother into the kitchen and as she helped her unpack the groceries she asked with the stony calm of despair, 'Just how deeply are you in debt to him?'

Rose responded indignantly. 'It's a perfectly legal loan! He was so kind when your father died—I don't know what I would have done without him. Alannah, your father's money was almost gone! Things had gone so radically wrong with everything that if Nick hadn't helped me I don't think I would have been able to keep going. But it's only a loan. Nick says that everything will come about again and we won't have to worry.'

'When did things start to go wrong for Daddy?'

Rose bent to slide the potatoes into the vegetable drawer. 'Well, a few years ago,' she said indistinctly. 'Not that it matters now. I trust Nick implicitly. He's immensely wealthy himself, you know. In an article in one of the newspapers a few weeks ago it said that he had the brains of a financial genius.'

And the heart of a stone. But Alannah did not say it aloud. Rose was determined not to recognise the true state of affairs and Alannah could not bring herself to force her mother to face facts. It would put an intolerable strain on their relationship. Pretty, silly Rose, Nicholas Challoner had called her; perhaps he was correct in his brutal summing up of her character, but she was the only mother Alannah had, and the future looked unbearably bleak. She did not want to drive her mother away by compelling her to feel guilt at her blithe manipulation of her daughter's life.

'He's very handsome, isn't he,' Rose chatted on, 'and with such incredible sex-appeal!'

'He wants to marry me.'

Rose nodded. 'I know. So romantic, Ally darling! He told me that he'd never forgotten you, even though he only saw you for those ten minutes or so that time.'

So that was how she was determined to see it. Well, she had always been romantic. Such a sentimental view of the situation was in keeping with her character.

Rose waited for an answer and when none was forthcoming asked with a touch of anxiety in her voice, 'What are you going to do?'

The new Alannah, this woman who felt so old that Rose was a child in comparison, said quietly, 'I'll marry him, I suppose.'

Rose didn't sigh her relief, but there was a note in her voice which made a lie of all her confident assertions. Rose, too, had been worried.

'I know you won't regret it,' she said quickly. 'He's a perfect gentleman, and although it sounds mercenary to say so, it will be just the sort of marriage I'd like you to make. He'll take good care of you all your life and you'll never have to worry about where the housekeeping money is going to come from. And, Alannah, it was he who paid for you to go to Switzerland.'

Alannah wasn't surprised. Everything she had learned today convinced her that Nicholas Challoner had been spinning a web about the Finderne family for years, ever since his wife died. 'And I suppose he's going to underwrite Trina's expenses at medical school.'

'Well, yes. And her fees at St Hilda's.' Defensively

Rose went on. 'Well, he offered and she would have been so miserable if I'd taken her away. She was doing so well there.'

Very carefully transferring eggs from the carton to the refrigerator, Alannah bit her lip. For a perilous moment her command of herself had slipped, revealing the secret Alannah, the terrified child who cowered beneath the calm mask. Her fingers trembled as she placed the eggs carefully into the rack. She fought down her instinct to scream and wail her misery and fear, to demand that her mother protect her from a future so empty of all that made life worth living that she could not bear to contemplate it. There was nothing she could do, nothing anyone could do. Nicholas Challoner had her backed into a corner and the only way she could maintain her courage was to hold her head high and refuse to let him see how abject her defeat was.

It was Trina who put her finger on the most painful spot. When told the news she had been quiet, her astonishment swiftly hidden, but that night at bedtime she followed Alannah into her room to ask without preamble,

'What about David?'

Alannah turned away from her, pulling her dress over her head. 'What about him?'

Trina sat down on the bed, regarding her gravely, 'Don't be silly, Alannah! He's expecting you to marry *him*, not Nick Challoner.'

Peering into the mirror of her dressing table, Alannah pretended to inspect her face. 'Nothing was said—no decision has been made.'

'Nothing needed to be said,' Trina returned impatiently. 'You're in love with him—he loves you. Don't try to lie to me, I was watching you at the party and it couldn't have been plainer. Is it money, Ally?'

'No.'

But Trina shook her head. 'It must be. You don't even know Mr Challoner. Ally, I don't have to go to med. school, you know.'

It hurt to lie to her sister, to see the clear green of her glance turn shadowy, even contemptuous, as she tried to convince her that Nicholas Challoner was what she wanted.

'If it's not money for us,' said Trina when Alannah had finished, 'it must be money for you. He's awfully rich, isn't he?'

'I believe so.'

Trina nodded. 'And David? What are you going to tell him?'

'I'll write to him tomorrow.'

'He'll be shattered.'

Alannah's smile was a bright mechanical movement of her mouth. 'No. He's so enthralled by this chance that his—his shock will soon be over.'

Perhaps Trina was fooled by that false brilliant smile. She frowned and sat silent for a moment before jumping up and saying urgently, 'Ally, he loves you. He's always loved you! Last year he didn't go out with anyone else, and he used to—I knew you weren't allowed to write to each other, so I used to read your letters to me out to him and he once said that he lived for those times. Ally——'

'You plead so ably for him that anyone would think you loved him yourself!' Alannah interrupted with harsh comprehension.

Flushing, obviously embarrassed, Trina held her sister's gaze steadily. 'I've loved him since I was a kid,' she admitted. 'But that's not important. Ally, don't marry Nick Challoner, just because he's rich! He frightens me—he's so cold and withdrawn! Even when he smiles his eyes stay hard and bitter.'

'He's absolutely seething with sex appeal,' Alannah pointed out indifferently. 'Don't worry about me,

Trina. Why don't you concentrate on David? I'll pass him on to you if you like, with my best wishes. Nothing better than keeping these things in the family, is there? So neat and tidy!' With a sudden squaring of her shoulders she turned to face her tormentor, her gaze hooded and opaque. 'I'm very tired, Trina. It's been a hectic day.'

'I can believe that,' Trina shot back. 'I don't suppose it's very often that you wave off the man you love and get engaged to the one you intend to marry all on the same day! Goodnight.'

When she had gone Alannah stood for long minutes staring at the door while her tired brain tried to make sense of the day she had just endured. It was useless; numbly she climbed into bed and lay awake for hours, her wide-open eyes staring into the night.

CHAPTER THREE

THEY were married ten days later. A very small wedding in a register office, with Rose and a silent Trina as well as the Richmonds, the couple he had taken her to see.

Alannah wore a dress of pale honeyed silk, exquisitely embroidered. It had been chosen by her mother at a very expensive boutique in the city. The dress emphasised the barbaric brilliance of her hair, and cosmetics supplied colour to her face; her hands and heart were as cold as ice.

She had seen very little of Nicholas in the intervening days. He had flown North, presumably to make arrangements for her reception at his house, only arriving back in Christchurch two days before the wedding.

Alannah wondered if he would make some gesture towards convention and escort her out, but except for one dinner with Trina and Rose at a very good restaurant he had made no effort in that direction. He didn't even attempt to see her by herself. Had he shouted it on the rooftops he couldn't have made his lack of interest more plain.

It was just as well. Not once had Alannah wept for the ruin of all her hopes, or bewailed her fate. The eager glowing girl was gone for ever, walled in behind battlements of ice. It did not occur to her that she was suffering from shock, and that he knew it. She did not even realise that such an attitude could not last. Floating, dissociated, she allowed Rose to make all of the arrangements. The only time she felt anything was when Nick put a splendid sapphire on her finger. Then she flinched.

Not so on her wedding day, a day chosen carefully by her, calendar and diary at hand, to fall right at the beginning of her fertile cycle. She hoped that for her conception would be easy and quick. She had no illusions about it being painless. Every time the cold green glance of her future husband rested on her the threat in it reinforced those he had spoken. He would make her pay and pay again until pain became commonplace.

She was composed though pale at her wedding, and when after a small celebration at the house it was time to go she put down an untouched glass of champagne and turned to her mother receiving her tearful embrace with gentle courtesy. Like many selfish people Rose was extremely sentimental.

But when Trina came up the two sisters exchanged a long glance before Trina whispered, 'Be happy, Ally,' and kissed her cheek.

In Alannah's heart something moved painfully. Since the engagement Trina had been so reserved that Alannah had accepted the fact of her alienation. Now it was clear that their deep mutual affection had not been overset by what her sister considered Alannah's defection.

'Alannah.'

At her husband's quiet command she moved away, touching Trina's hand with a tremulous smile before making her farewells to the Richmonds.

Outside Nick's hired car waited. Just before she got in Alannah turned and surveyed the gracious façade of her home, gave one last look at the garden and the view. Then she firmed her lips and waited while Nick closed the door. She did not look behind.

They were almost across the city, when he said, 'Our plane leaves in half an hour. Do you need anything?'

'No, thank you.'

'You're not curious about our destination?'

'Not in the least,' she said coldly, closing her eyes as she leaned back against the headrest. It was almost dark. Through the slightly opened window came the faint smell of coal. It was going to be a cold night.

He took her at her word, saying no more until they reached the airport. Even then they spoke only commonplaces. Once on the jet he opened a briefcase, busying himself with its contents. He read very quickly, skimming, occasionally making notes.

Alannah closed her eyes and tried to catch up on some sleep. The past week had not been exactly conducive to restful nights. Before long the drone of the big jets began to act as a lullaby, and she sank deeper and deeper into the seat, to wake some time later with a start at the touch of his hands.

'What——?' she began.

'Seatbelt,' Nicholas told her laconically, clicking it into place.

His profile was perfect, a miracle of lines and curves formed into a harsh beauty that attracted every feminine eye. When he looked at her she closed her eyes again, reluctant to let him see her unwilling appreciation. At the light touch of his mouth on hers her eyes flew open again to stare with blurred intensity into his sardonic face.

'We're nearly there, Alannah,' he said before he sat back and fastened his own belt.

As she had assumed, their destination was Mangere Airport in Auckland. When their baggage had been collected he led her out into the car park where an enormous Mercedes-Benz waited.

Alannah had visited Auckland before, but only twice. Ordinarily she would have been extremely interested in this sprawling, subtropical city set on its two harbours and dotted with little fairytale volcanic cones, most of them bearing traces of fortifications, the only remaining signs of the high Maori population in pre-European times. But tonight she stared ahead with dull eyes, apprehension and pressure beginning to force cracks in the wall of ice behind which she had retreated.

Tonight she would become Nicholas Challoner's wife, be forced to endure intimacies which she had only ever imagined in David's arms. Twelve hours from now she would be a virgin no longer and her husband's long exploitation of her body would have begun. As her eyes fell on his hands at the wheel she imagined them, cruel and persistent, on her skin, and shuddered, biting the inside of her cheeks to prevent the nervous trembling of her lips.

I hope it doesn't hurt, she thought, then, bitterly, *what does it matter if it does?* Plenty of other women before her had been in exactly this position. Why, in the Arab world today women were still married to men they had never exchanged a word with, never even seen before. She would not be the first to dread her marriage night, nor would she be the last.

And she did not want kindness or any consideration from Nicholas. While she hated him with this cold fervour she would maintain her integrity. He had said he did not want companionship or love or affection. Good, for he was not likely to get any of them. Let him find out what it was like to have a wife who suffered his presence only because she could not avoid it. With David there would have been tenderness and loving-kindness, laughter and quiet delight in each other's company, but when she was subjected to Nicholas Challoner's passion there could only be anger and cold disdain and a dumb acceptance of all that fate had chosen to throw at her.

They took the motorway which led them through the centre of Auckland to cross the Harbour Bridge. After several miles it dwindled down to an ordinary highway, heading north. Here it was quite dark and the scent from outside the car was that of the country and the sea combined. Headlights bored towards them, they passed through small villages and seaside towns until at last Nicholas made a right-angled turn and the big car swung quietly down a narrow country road.

Trees and red banks showed briefly in the lights as they wound up a hill. Another right-angled turn plunged them down through tall groves of manuka, the spicy brisk perfume familiar and dear.

At last the road flattened out, ran between paddocks then over a cattle-stop, and they were in an enormous brick forecourt. At the touch of his finger on a button on the the dash the garage door lifted.

'Welcome to Puhinui,' he said, coolly insolent as he leaned over and unlocked her door, pushing it open. Behind them the garage door closed.

A shiver ran up Alannah's spine. She waited until he had found the lights before she climbed from the car.

He waited, bored yet impatient, at a door. When Alannah came up he smiled and lifted her in his arms, saying above her head, 'One must observe tradition,' as he carried her into a wide passage and set her once more on her feet.

'Don't bother,' she snapped, pulling away from the hand that steadied her.

He shrugged but ignored her temper. 'I suppose you'll want to wash. This way.'

The house was modern, a sprawling place of white walls and brick floors, totally sophisticated yet warming her heart with its welcoming atmosphere. Had Ngaire Challoner accomplished this?

The bedroom was enormous, dominated by a huge fourposter bed hung with fabric the same pretty pink as the walls and the drapes. On the floor a carpet of deeper pink met Alannah's reluctant feet. It couldn't have been a greater contrast to what she had seen of the rest of the house, and somehow the two didn't go together, worldly ambience at odds with the soft, Colonial charm of the bedroom.

It cloyed. And it clashed with the smouldering red of her hair. Alannah tightened her lips as she put her handbag down on a chair, averting her eyes from the enormous bed as though it was an obscenity.

'The bathroom is through the middle door.' Nick gestured at three doors half hidden by a delicately carved screen. 'Do you want to shower?'

'Yes, thank you.' She heard her voice, thin and without emotion, say the words. 'If you'd put that bag on to something—thank you,' as he heaved it on to the bed.

He stood watching as she unlocked it and took out what she needed, choosing the first thing that came to hand to change into. Nicholas lifted his brows as she turned towards the bathroom, eyeing the dress she carried.

'No tantalising negligee?' he asked, the question a taunt. 'We'll be quite alone, you know.'

Instantly she stopped. 'Is that what you want me to wear? I believe my mother bought one or two. If that's what you need to stimulate your appetites then of course I'll oblige.'

She had intended her words to goad him, but instead of the reaction she expected she heard him laugh, softly and without humour.

'No, my sweet wife, I don't need such obvious provocation to rouse my passions. The look of you is quite enough. But yes, it pleases me to request that you wear something a little more bridal than that.'

Stonily, fighting down the nausea that clenched her stomach, Alannah crossed back to the case and with trembling fingers set down the green shirtwaister she had picked up. A short search discovered the glamorous robe her mother had bought her and its matching nightdress, all lace and silk in pure virginal white. Nicholas didn't move, but she felt his glance on her, diamond-hard, the pale green totally without softness.

Oh, David! her heart cried, but it was with a head held high that she walked behind the screen and into the bathroom. This too was hung with fabric, but in a shade of green.

To her surprise he left her to shower in peace. She had half expected him to follow her and pile humiliation on humiliation by forcing her to strip and shower in front of him, but apparently that was a little too obvious for him. The warmth of the water eased away the stiffness of the journey, but nothing, not the expensive scented soap or the enormous, warm bath sheet or the sybaritic luxury of her surroundings, could lessen the pain in her heart and the fear that whitened her face. Not for the world would she have him see that fear. After she had cleaned her teeth she used a lip-gloss on her pale lips and in a cloud of silk went back into the room.

Nicholas was standing by the window, staring out into the night. At her arrival he turned his head and looked her over, long and insolently, as she stood quietly in the centre of that lovely hateful room.

'I'll shower now,' he said at last, surprising her with the harshness of his voice. 'Your dressing room is through the next door.'

So she hung up her clothes and put away the exquisite underthings Rose had insisted on buying. It would not have surprised her to discover Ngaire Challoner's clothes still in place, but there was no sign that there had ever been a previous occupant.

The great length of hanging space and the drawers which filled one end of the room were empty. Of course the neatly embroidered lavender bags which lay scattered about might have been a whim of Ngaire's. If they were, they were a pleasant one, Alannah thought, turning one in her cold fingers. The tiny movement was caught by the wall of mirrors opposite her; she lifted her head and stared at her reflection. Not as pretty as Trina, he had said, and indeed she was not, for her eyes were too big and her features irregular; even her smile was lopsided. It was her hair which caught the eye, a mass of it, dark copper with gleams of gold and fiery red, tumbling about her small face almost as though invested with a life of its own.

I must get it cut and thinned, she thought with distaste. David had loved it like that, had delighted in running his hands through the clinging silk of it, but there was no longer any need to take notice of David's desires. She belonged to Nicholas Challoner now, signed, sealed and delivered. It would be easier if she thought of David as dead.

The hand shackled by a gold wedding ring clenched on the fragile little bag, crushing the dried stalks within to release more of the faintly musty, evocative fragrance. In the mirror her face looked pinched in the grip of an intolerable grief. Slowly, with an effort of will that held her rigid, she smoothed out the lines of anguish into a careful, blank mask. The muslin bag dropped to the floor. She picked it up and put it into the drawer before she went back into the bedroom.

Her husband was already there, clad in narrow black trousers and a black shirt. Alannah wondered if he had deliberately chosen to wear the colours of mourning and dread. It seemed very likely, as likely as that he had chosen to put her at a disadvantage by being fully clothed while she was humiliated by wearing clothes cleverly designed to reveal the desirability of the body beneath them.

As she came back into the room he looked up

sharply, subjecting her once more to that intent, insulting stare.

'Efficient, too,' he jeered, dumping the empty suitcase on to the floor at the foot of the bed. Very softly he said, 'Come here.'

The sickness which had threatened her before rose in her throat, but she came up to him, standing quietly as he lifted a hand and tilted her chin. Her lashes drooped so that all he could see was the stiff smooth mask and the line of lips tightly pressed together to hide their trembling.

A harsh sigh startled her into peeping beneath her lashes. He looked tired, the magnificent bone structure prominent beneath the dark skin.

'It doesn't have to be like this,' he said suddenly, unexpectedly.

A pulse beat heavily in her ears as her nausea was replaced by anger. How dared he think that he—that *anything* could make his actions less barbaric!

Very coolly she said, 'Yes, it does. Oh, you needn't worry that I'll fight you, or scream or do anything stupid. You're paying for me and I know how high the price is. I'll be a dutiful wife. But that's all I'll ever be.'

She lifted her lashes to reveal a blue blaze of hatred and he laughed, his expression demonic, and said thickly, 'So be it, my lovely. Let's see if you're over-priced, shall we?' as he hauled her against him.

A shaft of moonlight reached a silver finger across the room, touching the table beside the bed. It glowed lovingly on the small vase of roses somebody had put there, reached even further to the face of the clock. Before the light had been snapped off Alannah had noticed that clock; it was a delicate affair of rose and white enamel with a silver face, dainty, more like jewellery than a timepiece. But it told the time. Her dry, hot gaze rested on the face for several minutes until she recognised that it was two-thirty in the morning.

She had not slept, lying so still in the great bed that her body was aching and stiff, while snatches of thought whirled hideously around her brain. For a long while she had listened to an owl calling, 'More-pork, more-pork,' counting the times he called and the number of seconds between each call. Once or twice there had been a harsh shriek which meant that a pukeko was out and about; carefully she conjured up its image, long, lacquer-red legs, blue-black body, beak like a scarlet Roman nose and an absurd tuft of white feathers for a tail.

But morepork and pukeko had fallen silent and she was left with only the sound of Nicholas's breathing beside her. It was regular and deep, perfectly peaceful. Alannah winced while her stomach churned.

At last, impelled by necessity, she crept slowly and carefully from the bed. She only just made it to the bathroom.

After the bout of nausea she leaned weakly against the wall, head pressed back against it as her breathing steadied and the tumult in her stomach dissipated.

Very quietly she cleaned her teeth and washed her face. She was naked and she fancied that she could smell and feel his touch on her. Her teeth closed on her bottom lip; after a wary glance at the closed door she set her jaw and reached into the shower and turned it on.

As she soaped her wrenched body, relaxing under the sharp jets of warm water, she thought fatalistically, *Well, that's over. It will never be as bad as that again.*

And later, *Perhaps I'm pregnant already and there'll be no need for any further—anything further.*

For you could not call what had happened to her

making love. As her memory forced her to live the long minutes spent in his arms she shivered, but pride, cold and basic, straightened her shoulders, pulling her upright. Nicholas had taken her with nothing but his own desire to satisfy, using her with a brutal skill which revealed that he was infinitely practised in the art of seduction. For seduction of a kind it had been. Expecting callousness, the kind of violence she actually experienced had come as a complete surprise to her. It was as though he could not bring himself to rape her, as though he had to use his expertise to compel a response from her unwilling body.

As she had promised, she had not resisted, but her disdainful passivity had angered him into murmuring into her throat, 'So far, Alannah, you're infinitely too expensive. It will be interesting to see if you can keep it up.'

She had allowed him to do what he wanted, not flinching as his hands and mouth sought her most intimate places, fondling her as though he found her slender body infinitely pleasurable in his bed, in his arms. Like a stone she had lain, closing her eyes to block out the sight of him, trying to dissociate herself from what was happening to her. The thought of David she repressed entirely. Bitterly, with a savage revulsion at the betrayal, she realised after a while that her husband's slow passionate caresses were producing an insidious response. But only a physical one.

Even as the cold rigidity of her body loosened she told herself that she hated him, that the slide of his lips across her breast was completely distasteful to her, and knew that she lied. While she lay locked into an agony of loathing, her brain remained crystal clear, but her body played the traitor to her will. Despairingly she was forced to recognise that beyond and beneath her instinctive hatred of him there were deeper, stronger instincts. Although she refused to allow him admittance to her heart or her mind he already held the key to the physical responses of her body.

He knew it, too. Scornfully, averting her head, she thought that with his experience it was easy enough for him to recognise the quick heat in her blood, the threatening pulse as her heart began to race. And the other signs which his remorseless hands discovered as they touched and stroked and explored.

She expected triumph, but Nicholas remained alarmingly gentle, finding her mouth with his own and touching the tight length of it with the tip of his tongue.

The unexpected novelty of the caress frightened her. She stiffened, jerking her head away, but pitilessly he turned it back, forcing her to endure it as slowly, drowsily, he explored the soft depths of her mouth while his body hardened against her.

At her sides Alannah's hands clenched into themselves. She should have been repelled by the sensuous intimacy of his embrace, but beneath his hand her breasts seemed to expand, and when the slow gentle stroking moved from breast to hip and then to thigh a kind of sick excitement shafted through her. At last she was about to penetrate the mystery. The traitor in her body had responded to his blatant virility. It was all that she could do not to writhe against him and moan her surrender, fuelling her shameful desire with the erotic contact of his taut strong body. She was ready for him, her thighs loose and aching, a deep charge of unsatisfied longing between them.

Yet she lay still, reining in the responses she could not kill.

'Relax,' he breathed, but her attempt to remain in control kept her rigid.

When his leg parted hers and the driving strength of his body overwhelmed hers she gave a choking gasp and twisted in rejection, the heat in her blood turned to ice as he took her with a fierce mastery which added to her sense of betrayal by giving as much pain as it had promised ecstasy.

When he collapsed, breathing harshly, she found that tears were streaming down her face, although she wasn't sobbing.

After a moment he lifted himself on to the bed and said harshly, 'It won't hurt again.'

'I know.'

Something of her emotion must have shown, for he put his hand out and touched her shoulder. And when she winced he muttered an imprecation under his breath before saying with cold contempt, 'You can sleep now. I've had enough of you for the night.'

But it was he who slept and she who had lain awake for hours, staring into the dimness of the bedroom, hating herself for that involuntary betrayal. She had been so sure of herself. How could she have known that when he touched her she would be unable to control her response? Was she the sort of woman who could be had by anyone, or had he recognised a basic attraction between them and decided to take her because of it?

No, that could not be so, because that first time they had met he had been deeply sorrowing for poor Ngaire. And if her suspicions were correct it was immediately after that interview that he had set to work to ruin her father, with this night as his goal. So it would not have mattered whether he felt able to wrest a response from her or not. Ever since that first meeting he had intended her to end up in his bed.

Now, dry and somewhat soothed by the shower, she pushed the weary conjectures from her brain. She must get some sleep or she would be fit for nothing tomorrow, and she did not like the idea of Nicholas's knowing smile when he saw dark shadows under her eyes.

Moving gingerly, for she was bruised and aching, she pulled on the nightdress her mother had chosen so carefully and switched the light off. *Oh, God, make me pregnant,* she prayed.

Once back in the bed she froze, heart in her mouth as he turned and murmured something and flung an arm across her, pulling her to lie against him. For an age she lay waiting for him to wake, but slowly the breathing which stirred her hair regularised and she relaxed.

Quite clearly he was accustomed to sleeping with a woman. However deep and real his grief for his wife, he hadn't remained celibate in her memory.

On this distasteful thought she drifted off to sleep, hoping urgently that he had a regular sleeping partner, a mistress who would use up all his energies so that his reluctant wife didn't have to endure his painful embraces too often.

When she awoke she was alone in the huge bed. For some minutes she lay staring with wondering eyes at the pink and white pattern of the tester above her before she remembered where she was.

A painful colour flooded her skin. She turned her head, but relaxed immediately when she saw that the bed was empty except for her. It was after nine o'clock, the charming little clock told her, and someone had pulled back the draperies at one of the windows to reveal a great plate-glass sliding door masked by a drift of white silk that ballooned into the room.

Alannah slid upwards, trying to see what sort of day it was, but the soft inner draperies successfully hid whatever lay outdoors.

Yawning, she stretched, becoming aware of a not unpleasurable tingling in her limbs. Although she had lain motionless while Nicholas made love to her somehow she had stretched muscles not normally in use. *Probably*, she thought sourly, still disgusted with her body's treachery, *trying not to respond!* Her questing eyes sought confirmation of the night's events on her body, found it in smudges which would eventually become bruises.

This brought back unpleasant memories. To banish them she scrambled out of bed, made her ablutions, then pulled on jeans and a thin white tee-shirt which she had smuggled into her suitcase against her mother's instructions.

For a moment she hesitated, drawn by the sunshine outside. Curiosity impelled her across the room.

The door slid silently back to reveal a terrace, small and brick-paved. Although it was gay with creeping, flowering plants, it was the view which brought a swift, soft exclamation of wonder to her lips.

For Nicholas had built Puhinui by the sea; a second glance revealed that the glittering, sparkling waters were really an estuary. Positioned on a small headland thrust out at one end of a wide bay, the house overlooked a creamy-pink strand and steep green hills where sheep moved slowly in single file along unseen tracks, and wire fences strode almost vertically in straight, fearless lines.

Pohutukawa trees, glossy in the warm autumn sunlight, clung on all sides of the headland. A questing breeze caused a wave of silver to pass over them as the leaves turned to the sun. The trees were old and gnarled and formidable, their great branches making swooping statements against the brilliance of the water and the sky.

Across the estuary there were other beaches, other headlands, and the occasional square shape of a house. A small launch pulled out from a matchstick jetty, puttering pleasantly in the soft silence. When she looked behind her Alannah could just discern where the estuary met the sea between two long peninsulas.

It was a drowned river valley with islands and miniature gulfs and harbours, about a mile across, she judged, and then laughed, because she had no idea how wide the stretch of water was.

'In a better mood this morning, I see.'

Nicholas's voice prevented any further delight in this new world he had given her. She froze, turning her head as he stepped through from the bedroom bearing a loaded tray.

'It's very beautiful,' she said stiffly, while her colour ebbed, leaving her strained and tired-looking.

'Yes.' He set the tray down on a white table shaded by a sun-umbrella and pulled up a chair, wrought iron and elaborately moulded like the table, with a vivid blue and white cushion. 'Come and have some breakfast.'

Her appetite had fled with his appearance; she said 'No—I'm not——' and he said quietly,

'Alannah,' and after a quick look through her lashes at the chilling determination of his features she sat down on the pretty, too-fussy chair and stared at the tray.

It was hard to swallow with his eyes on her, but after a while she found herself enjoying superbly fresh flounder, although she could manage nothing else except a glass of fresh orange juice.

'Coffee?' At her quick headshake he asked, 'Pour me a cup, please.' And when she had done this he possessed himself of the hand which had given it to him and held it, looking down at the slender pale fingers.

A fierce wave of dislike washed over Alannah. It took all her self-command not to twist her hand and claw at him, mark him for life with her hatred. With his head slightly bent over her hand he looked like every woman's dream, handsome and sexy, carrying himself with smooth arrogance. For a moment her emotions flamed in her eyes, then as he looked up the thick screen of her lashes hid them.

His mouth hardened. 'All right, so you loathe me. I expected nothing else. But it doesn't have to be like that, Alannah. You could make a pleasant life for yourself.'

She lifted her brows. 'With you here?'

The long fingers tightened a moment, most painfully, on hers, then he returned her hand to her side of the table. 'Yes, with me here.' He leaned back in his chair, watching her with a kind of grim mockery which she found hard to face. 'You're an expensive little creature and with me you'll never be short of money. It's clear that you like the place. And if you give yourself half a chance you may find yourself liking me. Not immediately,' she made to refute his statement, 'no, I'm prepared to give you a few weeks to get over your sulks. But last night proved two things. One was that you were still a virgin.' He paused, but when she made no attempt to ask him what the other was, just stared at him with great resentful eyes, he continued, 'And the other is that you are not indifferent to me.'

'I've often been told that physical attraction is frequently divorced from all evidence of liking or respect,' she returned with exquisite courtesy. 'I believe it now. And I'm quite sure that what you got from me—all that you'll ever get from me—is no more than any other man who was young and personable and experienced could make me feel.'

'Such as the boy-friend?'

She shrugged, although the taunt was like a blow to her heart. 'As you discovered, I was still a virgin. David and I were prepared to wait.'

'Fortunately for you,' he returned, smiling unpleasantly. 'So you're determined to remain uncooperative?'

'I told you last night what I was prepared to do. I can see no reason why I should make things easier for you, just to assuage any feelings of guilt you may be suffering from.'

He leaned back in his chair, that ice-green gaze slipping over the pale contours of her face. 'You know very little about me if you think I suffer from guilt,' he informed her silkily. 'On the contrary; your aloofness I find a challenge. It will give me exquisite pleasure to touch you knowing that you hate me but love the touch.'

Her eyes flew to meet his. With a sick horror she saw calculated anticipation tighten his features as he stood and came to her and ran a finger over the tender junctions of forearm and upper arm. Beneath the soft touch her pulse flicked, and he laughed and held out his hand.

'Come,' he said softly. 'You've slept and eaten and had a shower. The rest of your day is mine, my sweet wife, like the rest of your life.'

As she rose he lifted her defiantly jutted chin and bent his head to bite the lobe of her ear, his arm around her shoulders preventing her swift recoil.

'My unwilling little slave,' he whispered, his breath warmly erotic as it tickled her ear. 'Mine to do exactly as I want with. Docile, I think was the word you used, wasn't it? Well, my docile wife, let's see how long you can keep it up.'

It was obvious that he was contemptuous of her strength of will. As he picked her up she held herself rigidly, rejecting the warmth and strength of his arms, the vital masculine scent and feel of him. No doubt he thought her a naïve, easily persuaded adolescent. He would, she vowed through set teeth as he stripped her, find out his mistake.

This time he was brutal, but her body accepted him without any of the pain of the night before. It took all her self-command to lie passive beneath him, but she managed it, refusing to do more than open her mouth for him. She could not prevent her breasts from tingling at his touch, and that treacherous need deep-buried in her loins from heating her skin and blood until she felt that she was on fire for him, but she was able to stop herself from giving any visible sign of her body's betrayal. Except for those he understood so well, the inevitable signs of readiness for his possession.

CHAPTER FOUR

WHEN it was over she lay breathing quickly, her eyes closed, hating him. She had read somewhere that most sex was in the head. As long as she hated Nicholas he could not wring the ultimate response from her. He had abducted her from her love, stolen her virginity, plundered her body, but while she hated him that was all that he could do. He would never watch her moan with ecstasy, never enjoy the triumph of taking her to paradise in his arms, all defences down, her surrender absolute and abject. And if the price she had to pay was frustration such as she felt now—well, she would pay it gladly.

'Look at me,' he commanded, and when she opened her eyes he was laughing at her, the hard handsome lines of his face creased in sardonic amusement. 'Such a stubborn little wife,' he taunted softly, his lips suddenly hungry at her breast.

Exhausted, Alannah said nothing, watching the dark head with wary antagonism. Not again, she thought—he can't, surely!

It seemed that he wanted only to torment her, because after a moment his mouth ceased its silken torture and he sighed.

'I'm tired,' he said in a surprised voice, and to her incredulous anger went to sleep, face pillowed against her soft curves, his naked body sprawled half across her in complete abandon. His weight was an oddly bearable burden.

How long she lay there contrasting the pale texture of her skin with his darkness she didn't know. At one stage she thought sleepily that although he possessed an enviable tan his skin was very smooth and fine. Of course up here in the north one had to be careful of too much exposure to the sun. That way lay skin cancer.

Then, shivering, headachy, she lifted herself up on an elbow. Nick was shrugging into trousers and she was cold because he had left her.

The glacial flames of his eyes swept her body, lingering with knowledgeable recollection on the sweet curves of breasts and hips and the long clean lines of her thighs. Alannah flung herself over on to her side, shamed and angered by his open assessment.

'Get up,' he commanded, and when she shook her head defiantly he came across and pulled her head out of the pillow, subjecting her to a long, probing look. 'Don't force me to force you to get up,' he said softly. 'It's well after midday and you look as though you could do with a brisk walk to drive away cobwebs.'

'I don't want to go.'

A muscle tightened in his jaw as he bent his head and kissed her defiant mouth, forcing it to open beneath his as he imposed his will on her. When he had finished he held her rebellious face still between his hands while their eyes met and clashed.

Alannah dropped hers first.

'Yes,' he said, nodding as though he could read her mind. 'Just do as I say and we'll deal quite well together, you and I.'

'Like hell!' Oh, how she wished she could copy the flat positiveness of his statement. It maddened her that the only note she could detect in her voice was defiance.

Into his face there flashed that hateful mockery, twisting his mouth into the smile that resembled a sneer. 'Like to bet on it? In five years' time you'll be smiling ruefully at all this waste of emotion.'

'Do you think so?' She looked her scorn, her glance

very level. 'If you honestly believe that you don't know me very well. Or is it that conceit is one of your strongest attributes?'

Prepared for the weight of his anger, she was surprised and irritated by his sudden burst of laughter.

'You'll be able to enjoy yourself finding out,' he said, releasing her. 'Come on, get dressed. Or do you want me to join you again?'

Her eagerness to get out of that hateful bed was unflattering if not insulting, but his only reaction was an ironic smile.

At least he left her alone while she picked up her scattered clothes and pulled them back on. Slowly, as if she had all the time in the world! It would do him good to wait.

So it was infuriating to find him reading beneath an umbrella on the little terrace, obviously not in the least annoyed.

Alannah stood quietly in the doorway watching him. He was extremely graceful, she thought as dispassionately as she could, with the grace of a hunting animal. With the sun gleaming redly on his dark slightly bowed head he was reading some great tome which looked extremely technical, the cold, haughty face absorbed in it.

This man, she thought strangely, knows all there is to know about me—about my body. It was an odd sensation, physcial as well as mental. The long fingers turning the pages could be both gentle and fierce, stroking her skin as though he was in love with the feel of it, holding her captive while he gasped out his ecstasy, using her as a receptacle for the children he wanted.

A billow of white silk caught across her face, clinging like a live thing until she brushed it away. It reminded her of the woman who had shared the bed with him before, the woman her carelessness had killed. Did he pretend that she was Ngaire come back to him when he took her in Ngaire's bed?

The thought revolted her. It was frightening enough to be the object of such impersonal lust, but to be used as a substitute, to know that while he enjoyed her another woman's face was imposed over hers, made her stomach churn.

Yet why should she care? On the day she died she would despise Nicholas; nothing he could do would ever erase her memories of the insults he had heaped on her. Still, it was with something almost like relief that she recalled that during their lovemaking his fingers had played with her hair as though the heavy curls pleased him, that he called her by name and whispered compliments about her face and body. As far as physical attributes were concerned she and his former wife shared nothing. Ngaire had been taller with long pale gold hair drawn back from beautiful, gentle features. There was a photograph of her on the chest of drawers in the bedroom and after the accident several had been published in newspapers. The refined patrician features were engraved on Alannah's brain.

'Ready?' he asked without lifting his eyes.

Nodding, she came out through the door into the sunlight, warm, flowing like a blessing over them both.

From the terrace steps led down through a thick bank of wildly tropical-looking plants to a lawn where a path took them beneath an enormous pohutukawa to the beach. It was narrow but safe, and Alannah was thankful that Nicholas made no offer to hold her hand or support her in any way, although he did go in front.

Then the beach, a pinky-cream curve of sand backed by a low bank overgrown with more pohutukawas, and beyond them a wide half circle of flat land rising abruptly to green hills. The water glistened and sparkled in the sunlight, dancing in tiny waves across the estuary, so still the air that she could hear the high whine of a chainsaw miles away. Across the water the farmlands were tree-shaded, green and strong and beyond them ran a line of hills. If you were used to having the Southern Alps as a backdrop these were nowhere near high enough to be called mountains, but they were beautiful too, their heavy covering of trees coloured misty blues and purples by distance.

Insensibly Alannah's spirits began to lift. At home in Christchurch the year had said goodbye to summer, but here it seemed almost warm enough to swim. A short paddle disabused her mind of that notion however, but everything was beautiful, so clean and fresh, and through the gap of the mouth of the river she could see white wings at sea, so many that she was moved to exclamation.

'You're looking at the Hauraki Gulf,' her husband told her. 'Some days during the holidays it seems that every Aucklander has a yacht.'

'Have you?'

He shook his head. 'I enjoy sailing, but I don't have enough time to spare to make one worthwhile.

Well, that sounded hopeful. Perhaps something in her expression gave her away, because he added with cutting emphasis, 'However, I intend delegating more responsibility so that when I have a family to come home to I can give them as much attention as I feel they need.'

And he picked up the hand swinging loosely at her side and kissed the tips of her fingers, his eyes coldly sarcastic.

After that they walked silently along the beach, Nicholas matching his steps to hers, looking around him with eyes half shut against the glare, his pleasure in his surroundings palpable.

You're getting too conscious of the man, Alannah told herself sternly. *Ignore him. He's ignoring you. Enjoy this beach, this scenery, this salty drowsy tingle in the air, the distant call of a gull....* She bent and took her sandals off and ran down towards the sea, impelled by some warning instinct to get away from him. The water was cool, not cold as she had first thought, and it played over her slender ankles and feet with a lover's caress. A sudden splash out in the bay made her start.

'A fish,' he informed her laconically. 'They jump quite frequently. Probably mullet or piper.'

Well, of course, what else could it be? She asked, 'Who looks after the house?'

'Ellen Thurkettle is our housekeeper. She lives with her husband in a flat behind the house. The farm manager lives in the cottage just beyond the cattle stop. You can see it——' He turned her and pointed to where the thin line of the road ran across the flat before climbing swiftly to the top of the ridge. 'There,' he said.

It was substantial, tree-embowered, and above a terrace great clumps of some pink flowered vine hung from a pergola.

'Ellen isn't easy to get on with,' he resumed, 'but she has integrity.'

'Something her employer lacks,' Alannah retorted with smooth malice.

He smiled, although his voice remained cold. 'Perhaps,' he agreed. 'What exactly are you complaining about? I gave you a choice.'

'An impossible choice! You knew perfectly well that I'd be obliged to agree to your proposition.'

'As I remember it, it was a proposal, not a proposition.'

'I would have preferred a proposition. You used your power to force Daddy into a situation he couldn't avoid. When he died you coaxed Rose into trusting you and got her further into trouble. You stole—and you intend to keep on stealing. You've stolen my virginity, you intend to steal my body to carry your children—you've stolen my life!' Sunlight rioted in the heavy curls as she flung her head back, holding his gaze with her own turbulent, scornful one. 'But you will never steal my heart, or my mind. They're still mine, well guarded. And there's nothing you can do about that.'

'There's nothing I care to do about it,' he said insolently, taking her hand and pulling her up into his arms. 'Do you think I care about your heart—or your mind? The only interest I have in either is that your intelligence makes you a suitable mother for those children you're so scathing about. As for your heart——' He stopped, and spread his hand out over her slight breast where her heart beat swiftly and painfully. 'That's the only thing that interests me about your heart,' he said, smiling at the wild frustration in her expression. 'That it beats double time when I touch you.'

'Fear.'

'Rubbish. Your pride won't let you admit it, but you want me. Oh, you put up a very good front, all patient resignation and sighs, but I don't have to work very hard to rouse you. Your body betrays you, you little fool. Do you think it would have been quite as painless last night—or this morning—if you hadn't been ready for me? You——' He caught her wrist only just in time, held it for several shattering, painful moments an inch from his face, and then bent his head and bit her hand just below the palm. The slender fingers tensed, then trembled, and he gave a soft satisfied laugh.

'You see?' he taunted, drawing her stiff arm down. 'You can't deny it, my lovely.'

'I hate you!'

'I know.' He began to walk again, holding her hand so that to anyone who watched it must have seemed as if they were walking in affectionate contact. 'Hate away, Alannah. I'd rather that than the dull indifference you try so hard to project. The only person you're hurting by your determination not to surrender is yourself. I enjoy you just as much; in fact, it gives me an added pleasure to watch you strive so hard for passivity when your body shakes with desire and welcomes me with almost indecent haste.'

'Stop it!'

'Then don't provoke me,' he said thinly, releasing her. 'I don't care if you lie like a log in my arms, you stupid little bitch. But I have no intention of allowing you privileges you don't deserve just because we make love together—or because you are my wife. If you want consideration from me you'll have to earn it.'

By now she had recovered some of her self-control. 'As Ngaire did?'

'Ah, but I loved Ngaire,' he retorted brutally. 'And that will be an end to that subject. I don't ever want to hear her name on your lips again. Understand?'

The naked ferocity in his face and voice frightened her. She twisted away from him, nodding, despising herself for her cowardice but unable to overcome it. He looked like a devil, the arrogance of his expression so harsh that for a moment she thought he might be driven to violence.

'You needn't worry,' he said contemptuously, 'I've never had to hit a woman and I certainly don't anticipate having to use force with you.'

'I told you that you won't need to,' she said tonelessly. 'You have two hostages—three, if you count David.'

'Another name I don't want to hear.'

By now she was shaking inside, heartsick and angry at her humiliation. 'Are there any others?' she asked with distant politeness.

As she turned her back to him a hawk swooped across the sand, the fierce predator's eyes searching out prey, the slow graceful glide lyrical as poetry. Alannah shivered.

'I'd like to go back now,' she said in a hard voice.

'Of course.' He looked at her slenderness and said without emotion, 'Although the temperatures up here are higher than in Christchurch you'll be wise to take a jacket wherever you go. It is autumn.'

Alannah nodded. She was suddenly overtaken by a vast tiredness. Not only had the tension of the last week strained her nerves, but Nicholas's savage possession of her had sent her into mild shock. Her body ached and the altercation had brought on a dull throbbing in her temples. She wanted nothing more than to sleep for a week—alone—and wake up back in her bed at home.

Once inside the house he surveyed her with the cool insolent stare she loathed because it made her feel small and stupid and inferior.

'Can you cook?'

Astounded by the irrelevance of his question, Alannah retorted, 'Yes.' Adding after a moment, 'Superbly, but with a limited repertoire so far.'

'Then you can prepare dinner, as I've given Ellen the weekend off.' He smiled, that hard, humourless movement of his mouth. 'One must observe the conventions, after all, and this is the only honeymoon you're likely to have. I have a few things I want to do first; when I've finished I'll come and help you.'

Alannah moved away, looked at him with frigid dislike. 'You needn't bother. I'm sure that I can find it on my own.' She smiled sweetly. 'After all, it's not as though the house is as big as Buckingham Palace.'

'Indeed it's not,' he returned softly, his expression icily controlled.

Well, no, it wasn't, but big enough. It took her a

few minutes to find the big, superbly equipped kitchen, and then a few more to discover where the food and utensils lived.

But she managed, as she must manage from now on in this cold empty life to which a moment's negligence and a man's vengefulness had condemned her. Blinking fiercely to chase away a few scalding tears, she opened one door of the immense refrigerator. Crying would not help, nor would self-pity. From now on she would have to concentrate on growing as hard a shell as that which made Nicholas impervious to any of the gentler emotions.

Her discovery of veal steak decided her on a menu; a foray into the large cool pantry nosed out the ingredients for borsch, a soup which had always been one of her favourites. The veal she would serve as a Stroganoff. For pudding she decided on another old favourite, apples baked with a stuffing of honey and dates and walnuts.

It was soothing to wash the apples and set them aside with the other ingredients, soothing to chop beetroot and apple for the borsch before setting it to cook in the stock she had found frozen in the deep-freeze.

When she had finished the preparation she left the kitchen, now warm with the good smell of food, and walked quietly back through the house, admiring its splendid lines and spaces with an appreciative eye.

In their bedroom Nicholas was transferring the contents of his pocket to the trousers he had just put on, absorbed in the small task. His hair was sleek from the shower, his expression at once more remote yet more familiar than she had ever seen it before. Just so had her father done some small task, putting his whole heart into it as he had with everything he did.

For the first time since Holt Finderne's death Alannah did not feel the familiar desolation. Instead there came the faint twist of amusement which this absorption had always caused. An amusement which was transferred to this man who was now her husband.

As quickly as it came she banished it. Start softening towards him and heaven knew where it might lead, possibly to liking, or even more dangerous things.

'Dinner will take about twenty minutes,' she told him politely on her way to the dressing room.

If he answered she didn't hear; when she returned from her shower, dressed and made up, the room was empty.

But after they had eaten he led her back into that big bedroom and once more in the cool, scented night he took her, pleasuring himself in the soft warmth of the body he had enslaved as surely as if he had loaded her limbs with chains.

Afterwards she touched with a finger the spot on her lip where she had bitten through the skin as she concentrated on keeping her body still and passive beneath his skilful lovemaking. If it killed her, she vowed, she would show him nothing but disdain. And on this second night of her marriage, as on the first, she prayed to be pregnant.

When she awoke the next morning she was alone once more in the bed. She had dreamed of her father and she awoke smiling, a hand outstretched. Then remembrance shadowed her face. The smile faded and she turned, dragging her upper arm over her eyes to hide the room from them.

From the end of the bed Nicholas said harshly, 'Time you got up, unless you want me to join you.'

'Now, you know better than that,' she retaliated, unbearably angered by her complete lack of privacy. It seemed that he invaded her dreams even as his virile body invaded hers, stamping her with the brand of his possession, forcing her to accept her slavery without making any attempt to escape it.

Hating him, she was afraid of him and the sensual power he had over her. When he touched her with those lean strong hands she shivered, her skin tightening, but it was not because he made her flesh crawl. That entirely involuntary reaction was one of sexual anticipation, and she despised herself for it. That dumb response was a betrayal of everything she had ever surmised about relations between the sexes.

So she turned her face away, preferring his anger to his lust, innocently unaware that one could be expressed in the other.

Beneath his breath he laughed, sliding his arm beneath the sheet to pass his hand over the slender contours of her body. Rigid, impotently angry at the slow pulse of excitement rising through her veins, Alannah winced as the heat that followed his hand suffused her skin. Her arm pressed so hard against her closed eyes that she could see white lightning flashes across the blackness.

'You should have jumped out immediately you woke,' he whispered, bending low so that the soft words were little sensations on her lips.

Alannah forced herself to relax, willing her outrage to die, waiting for his mouth to plunder hers. His hand stopped at her waist, then explored her navel in a movement so subtly sensual that she felt colour scorch upwards. He was close, she could sense his presence with the skin of her face, yet he did not kiss her, and when anticipation forced her to drag her arm away he was smiling, his head turned so that he could see the slight mounds of her breasts, their taut tips signalling her arousal.

As if conscious of her scrutiny he looked her full in the face, that strange set smile turning his features into an antique mask of lust.

'You're a liar,' he said conversationally as his hand

moved lower, probing yet infinitely gentle, proving just how much of a liar she was.

Yet even through the heated hunger of her body her will held firm.

'What you get from me you could get from a prostitute,' she retorted, her voice clear and cold. 'A reluctant acquiesence, that's all. I despise you—I always will.'

'How often do I have to tell you that I don't care?' The hard scorn of his tones was strangely at variance with the seductive caress of his fingers. It was as if they were two different people, the physical part separated completely from the brain and the emotions.

Rose had said once that such a separation was easy for men, that was one of the great differences between the sexes. Alannah could hear her light, clear cultured voice now. 'Women,' she had said oracularly, 'must love to be able to give themselves fully.'

Perhaps for most women that was true; but her daughter knew that the perilous enchantment of physical ecstasy was only prevented by her determination not to surrender. Instinct warned her that if once she relaxed she would be totally subjugated, forced into even harsher slavery by the weakness of her own body. The only way she could keep her integrity intact was to resist to the last this blazing power her sexuality wielded over her will and her brain. So she closed her eyes once more and began reciting her times tables, and if she lost her place for a long time somewhere in the middle at least Nicholas didn't know.

'So obedient,' he said brusquely, when it was over. 'Like a puppet.'

She opened her eyes wide, staring into the dark features with false surprise. 'But that's what I am,' she said intensely, her mouth compressed in bitterness.

'You and Rose pulled the strings and I was jerked into position. If you'd wanted a loving wife, Nick, you should have gone about things a different way.'

He shrugged and leaned up on an elbow so that he could see better into her face. 'And would I have won you if I'd courted you in due order?'

'No,' she said coldly. 'I love David.'

The long fingers traced from the line of her jaw to the full red outline of her mouth, probing within a sensual invasion which infuriated its unwilling recipient.

'Do you?' he mused, laughing down at her. 'I don't think so, my sullen little termagant. If you really loved him you wouldn't be lying here resenting the fact that I can arouse you. Hero-worship is a potent emotion, but it fades. Admire your shining knight by all means, provided you face facts. And the fact you had better face first of all is that for better or for worse, you're mine. You've determined that it should be for worse; quite frankly I don't care one way or the other except for the purely selfish reason that a complacent wife makes a pleasanter companion than one who sulks and spits. But,' his voice hardened into icy purpose, 'whichever way you choose to behave, you redheaded shrew, there's no escape. I own you. I bought you, paid highly for you, and I intend to get the most use out of that delectable little body that I can.'

Every word that he said was reinforced by the contemptuous sweep of his eyes, the cold possessiveness of the hand that travelled the length of her body to come to rest where the swift beat of her heart thundered between her high breasts.

Alannah clenched her fists, desperately striving for the control not to slap his dark, gloating face until his ears rang.

His low laughter almost forced her over the edge, but although her face whitened with the effort she knew that her usual fiery response would be playing into his hands.

'Learning some discretion at last?' he jeered, and laughed again at the blazing fury she dared not express. 'In five years' time when I have you well and truly cowed I think I'll miss our battles. They give a spice to life rather like the joys of the hunt.'

His lips touched hers, tantalising, seducing, but when she refused any response he swooped, teasing the high peak of her breasts until the nipple hardened in his mouth. Then, satisfied, he grinned at her open anger and chagrin.

'One of the reasons I'm going to enjoy your body so much is that it doesn't even try to lie,' he said, and with infuriating familiarity slapped her lightly on the tight, flat plane of her belly. 'Now, get a baby tucked away in there and you'll make me very happy.'

'I hope I'm unable to have children,' she retorted in tones which trembled with outrage.

For a moment something ugly showed in his face. It was swiftly hidden by the bland expression he could assume at will.

'If that happens, my love, I'll divorce you and marry someone who's already proved her fertility.' He kissed her, hard, and whispered into her ear, 'But I'll keep you as my mistress, incarcerated in a luxurious prison just for my pleasure.'

Sheer horror dilated her eyes. 'You wouldn't—you *couldn't*!' she stammered, wincing as he bit the lobe of her ear.

'No?' He drew back and looked into her pale face, smiling in a way that frightened her even further. 'Just hope and pray that my child gives signals of its advent fairly soon. I'm not getting any younger. Now get up. Ellen will be here and you'll have to meet her some time.'

Ellen Thurkettle was a thin woman, several inches

taller than Alannah and with one of the most uncompromising faces the younger woman had ever seen. One quick, all-seeing glance and Alannah felt that she had been weighed and found very much wanting. The housekeeper did not even smile as she shook hands and the look she bestowed on Nicholas was frankly condemnatory.

'You might have let me know,' she said crisply.

Nick shrugged, 'Why? The house is always in perfect condition, if that's what's worrying you.'

'You know it's not.' The sharp glance swung back to Alannah. 'Well, I don't know what you're up to, Nick, but I hope you do.'

'Of course I do.' The words were delivered in his blandest voice.

Again there lanced that swift sharp look at her employer's new bride. 'I'll take you over the house after you've had breakfast, Mrs Challoner.'

'Call her Alannah,' Nick instructed.

'It's her privilege to tell me that.'

Nick's eyes lingered a moment too long on the soft bruised fullness of Alannah's mouth. 'Darling?' he drawled.

'Please do.' Making her voice as cool and uncaring as she could, Alannah met the other woman's eyes. 'If—now that we're to—to share the house it will make things easier.'

The hint of appeal in her words met with no response. 'I'm quite happy to call you Mrs Challoner if that's what you'd prefer,' the housekeeper said inflexibly.

Nicholas sighed. 'Don't be silly, Ellen. You called Ngaire by her first name without any qualms, you can do the same for Alannah. Now what's for breakfast?'

Orange juice, eggs and kidneys, porridge and a cold cereal, beautifully served in a small annexe off the dining room with the sun streaming in across the floor in glowing golden warmth and through the long sliding door a view out on to another terrace gay with flowers. Beyond it was the estuary, glinting through the heavy branches of the pohutukawas like a million jewels.

Almost insensibly Alannah felt a lift of her spirits. The worst must be over. Although Nicholas had made himself master of her body and her life her integrity was still intact.

A curious tightening down her backbone made her concentrate fiercely on the food. Surely she would become accustomed to his lovemaking, so that, even though she would never like it, she would be able to ignore its threat. At the moment she was too conscious of the man across the small round table. Even with her lashes hiding her eyes she could observe the movements of his hands, the spare lean strength of them, and recall only too clearly how they had traced out her body with lingering, sensual thoroughness.

That must diminish. Old married couples did not spend all their life in a state of quivering awareness of each other. And when she had developed a suitably distant outlook then the natural beauty of her surroundings would give her constant pleasure.

After a mostly silent breakfast Nicholas closeted himself in his office while the rigidly disapproving Mrs Thurkettle took Alannah around the house with an elaborate formality which at first amused her, then, when her overtures were politely rebuffed, irritated her so much that in turn she developed a cold reserve to hide her emotions.

But not even the housekeeper's attitude could prevent Alannah's appreciation of her new home. Whoever had designed it had been a genius, blending the structure into its surroundings so that from the outside it looked an organic part of the landscape. Inside his statements had been more startling, attracting the eye with their boldness yet always immensely satisfying in form and balance. Skilfully he had woven different levels together to take advantage of the slope back to the mainland, skilfully contrasted open spaces and enclosed areas to meet every need of the people who lived there.

It was big, far bigger than she had realised. Beyond their room was a whole nursery suite, bedrooms, bathrooms and what would be a beautiful playroom. There were guest rooms, restrained yet dramatic, opulent enough to satisfy the most demanding visitors. As well as the formal sitting room and dining room there were others, a library and music room, a small morning room furnished in cane and facing north-east to catch the sun.

When Mrs Thurkettle went back to her kitchen Alannah made her way outside and explored the gardens thoroughly, discovering a heated pool set in an enormous atrium which would make summer entertainment simple and glamorous, and a tennis court behind high netted walls overgrown with passionfruit vines, still heavy with round wrinkled fruit.

Like a child Alannah bit into one, enjoying the sweet-sharp pulp with its multitude of glistening black seeds before throwing the rind into a convenient orange tree. Its fruit was swelling but still hard and green; it would be some months before it was edible. But there were others, several different sorts of lemons, and apple trees hung with carefully thinned fruit, huge green Granny Smiths and a tree which held apples like gold and red globes. When Alannah bit into one the flesh was so crisp that she smiled, fantasising about small explosions between her teeth.

Apparently Nick subscribed to the idea of self-sufficiency, for the orchard was large as well as being well cared for. Separated from it by a hedge of feijoa trees was a kitchen garden. After a guilty thought about the imminence of lunch Alannah picked up a feijoa fruit like a knobbly green egg, and enjoyed its unusual pineapple-peach flavour, licking her fingers with relish when she had finished it.

A man was hoeing between rows of broccoli, a tall, thin, lined man who gave her a startled look as she came towards him.

When she bade him good morning he nodded, replying briefly, 'Morning.'

'I'm Alannah—Challoner,' she said as she offered him her hand, hoping that he hadn't heard that momentary hesitation.

'Hugh Thurkettle.' He looked at her slender fingers doubtfully, then shook hands. 'Hope you'll be very happy,' he said, flushing slightly.

Alannah felt her own colour rising. It was with a stilted air that she replied. 'Thank you; I've been exploring. What a superb garden! Do you do all of it?'

He continued hoeing but said, 'Yes.'

'The garden round the house too?'

'Yes. Nick knows what he wants. I do it.'

The sun caught in Alannah's hair as she bent to pull a small weed. When she straightened up a sudden wave of giddiness made her shake her head. 'Oh dear, I stood up too quickly. Mr Thurkettle, are those guavas at the end of the garden?'

'Yes. Yellow and red. Not ripe yet—another couple of months.'

She nodded. 'It's a wonderful place, isn't it? So quiet and beautiful.'

'That's so,' he said, and surprisingly, 'You'll like it here.'

Perhaps he felt he had been over-communicative, because from then on she could only get monosyllables for answers. After a while she gave up and wandered back to the house through a path between sweetly scented borders.

For a long time she sat on a lounger beside the pool. Both Thurkettles were dour and far from communicative, but when confronted with a direct question Ellen had answered equally as directly. So Alannah knew that although a decorator had been hired for the rest of the house, Ngaire had furnished the bedroom herself. She must have felt ill at ease with the clean modernity of the rest of the house to have used such an opposing style in the one room she had tackled.

Alannah sighed and dipped her fingers into the water. To her initial surprise it was warm enough to swim in.

Well, of course it would be heated. Why not? As Rose had told her, Nicholas was rich.

'Solar panels.' His voice came from behind her, the mocking inflection stiffening her shoulders.

'So—oh, I see.' Automatically her eyes searched the roof looking for the square panels which so many new houses were sporting.

'They face north,' he told her, and held out his hand. 'Have you been down to the boat shed?'

'No.' Avoiding his hand, she scrambled to her feet, but he smiled and slid his arm around her waist, holding her close.

'Then let's go down,' he said pleasantly.

The boatshed was at the foot of the cliff, a sturdy structure with a slipway across the narrow ledge of rocks to deep water. The green walls sheltered a small runabout, a dinghy and two canoes as well as the interesting assortment of gear all the best boatsheds acquire over the years, crayfish pots, strong-smelling nets, long spears and an assortment of fishing lines and hooks, very aged sandshoes and even a pair of ancient black togs hung up on a nail.

'It looks bare.' Alannah's voice sounded odd in the big, shadowed space.

Nicholas had released her and was checking over a crayfish pot.

'It was built in the days when boats were kept indoors, that's why it's the size it is.' He moved away, hands in pockets and stood staring at the runabout. 'This afternoon we'll go across to the other side.

'Shouldn't you be working?' she queried.

'Worried about my income?' The taunt made her stiffen, but without a pause he continued, 'Don't worry, madam wife, I'll make sure that you don't ever have to worry about money. The business won't die just because I'm on my honeymoon. I delegate responsibility and I trust those I employ. This week I am entirely at your disposal.'

'If you were you'd drown,' she said with caustic emphasis.

He laughed at that and came across to where she stood, a slim, defiant little figure with hard eyes, the normal softness of her mouth compressed into a thin line, her chin lifted to reveal the faint cleft in it.

'You'd be the merriest of all merry widows, wouldn't you?' he jeered softly as he grasped her shoulders and pulled her against him. 'Sorry my darling, I have no intention of dying so conveniently. You'll have to put up with my distasteful authority over you and your life for many years to come.'

And to make sure she got the message he kissed her, deliberately using his strength to enforce the not so subtle threat of his words.

That day set the pattern for the days which followed. They walked, exploring the farm, and often he took her out in the runabout to small bays and large, ranging the length and breadth of the estuary, conversing at first stiffly, later with increasing ease while he showed her the teeming natural life which was spread out so richly about the estuary.

The days weren't so bad. It was the nights Alannah dreaded, for each one that passed made it harder to lie passively in his arms. Not that her lack of response annoyed him. He seemed to get a perverse pleasure from her mute resistance, taunting her with the small betrayals of her body until his desire peaked and for too short a time that infuriating self-control was eclipsed by a towering rush of passion which left him relaxed and satisfied.

He enjoyed imposing his will on her, but at least he didn't rape her quickly. No, she thought cynically, he was too much of an artist for that. Some strain of egoism made it necessary for him to have a receptive partner. And he enjoyed the smooth satin of a woman's body, the shape and texture of it, the scent and taste of it, for when he made love he told her so, using his voice to reinforce his physical mastery until her body began to accept his possession with acquiescence, a guilty, secret pleasure.

Not her mind, though. Each night the burning resentment in her eyes made him laugh jeeringly as slowly he began to prepare her for his conquest. But, in spite of her body's weakness she denied him the ultimate satisfaction, refusing to submit to the little death she had read about.

When the week he had allotted to a honeymoon was gone Nicholas left each morning for Auckland and Alannah found herself with the whole day ahead of her, free. She made no more overtures to Ellen Thurkettle, contenting herself with keeping their suite clean and tidy.

Often she worked in the garden, weeding and helping the silent Hugh, and at the weekends she did all of the cooking, startled to find that she enjoyed it.

No visitors came; they might have been stranded on

an island, so completely cut off was she from the life of the surrounding district. And once she had run out of the money in her bank account Alannah didn't know how she was going to manage, as Nicholas never mentioned it. No doubt he had accounts at the local stores; she was not going to ask Ellen about that sort of thing.

Perhaps he wanted to keep her barefoot and pregnant, she thought as she sealed the envelope of a letter to her mother. Or perhaps he had too many other things on his mind to care about a penniless wife. Certainly he spent long hours in Auckland, then often retired to his office after dinner, not coming to bed until long after Alannah was asleep.

But he never failed to wake her.

CHAPTER FIVE

THEN one evening she couldn't face the coffee after dinner. The rich odour brought sudden nausea to clog her throat. For long moments she sat staring into the cup while certain other happenings fell into place in a pattern.

Nicholas was sitting opposite her, for once relaxed on the pale sofa in the music room while they listened to Janet Baker and James King singing Mahler's *Das Lied von der Erde*. He was one of the few people she knew who really concentrated on listening to music, his expression absorbed and reflective, no book on his lap or movements revealing boredom. Afterwards he would discuss it with her; usually she listened resentfully until her latent interest made her forget her wrongs. Once or twice she had found herself enjoying their exchanges. But not tonight. Moving as inconspicuously as possible she took her coffee back to the kitchen, washed the cup and put it away. Not for anything would she let him know her conclusions. It might be petty to deprive him of the pleasure her condition would bring him, but that was exactly how she felt.

A week later she left the doctor's surgery, small, pale and indomitable. Hugh had driven her into the nearest town, after explaining selfconsciously that she wasn't to use the car.

'Nick said you're not used to our bad roads,' he muttered.

Alannah smiled. Nick had said no such thing, but she respected Hugh for trying to soften the blow.

'He's right there,' she said, adding, 'I don't want

him to know about this. It's—well, I want it to be a surprise.'

He had looked doubtful, but her destination reassured him. Now, with the sky darkening into dusk, she leaned back in the seat and watched the landscape.

So now she knew.

Deep in her body there lived an alien, a parasite who drew on the resources of her being, whose presence caused this constant nausea.

Yet she was thankful for it, even smiling as the car rattled over the cattle-stop. With his purpose accomplished Nicholas would have to leave her alone now.

The other big car was in the garage, but there was no sign of him in the house. Not that Alannah went looking for him; she only just made the bathroom in time and was still sitting on the side of the bath when his step sounded in the bedroom beyond.

'Alannah?'

Before she had time to answer he was in the bathroom, an oddly arrested expression on his face as he saw her, pale and shaken, her face pinched in the aftermath of nausea.

'What is it?' he demanded.

Alannah stood up. 'I'm pregnant,' she answered, suddenly savagely, viciously angry with him. Her only dreams of pregnancy had been in connection with David; she wanted to hurt Nicholas as he had hurt her, trample on his dreams as brutally as hers had been crushed.

'I see.' The words came slowly as his expression cooled into impassivity.

Well, what had she expected? Nothing more than this bloodless acceptance, so why did it add fuel to the flames of her temper?

'And I don't feel well,' she snapped, arrogance colouring her voice. 'Will you leave me alone, please?'

He smiled and came into the room, holding out his hand. 'Come on, you little shrew, I think you need to go to bed. You look like death.'

His calm refusal to respond to her provocation brought her to boiling point. When he went to slide his arm around her waist she struck him away, hurting her hand against the hard muscle and sinew, in some perverse way enjoying the pain.

Beneath that deep tan he went white, his anger so palpable that for a moment Alannah's own fury wavered.

Before she could lose it entirely she rushed into speech. 'I'm pregnant, didn't you hear? You've accomplished what you married me for, so I don't need to suffer your repulsive touch any more. At least, not until you decide you want another child. My flesh crawls whenever you touch me. Just leave me alone, will you! I hate you!'

For one terrifying moment she thought she had gone too far. Nicholas stared at her with such savage intensity that her hands on the edge of the bath whitened as she gripped it. A muscle flicked by his mouth, a tiny movement obvious in the mask of his face.

Then, slowly, he subdued that first blind fury, although his voice was quick and vicious as a whiplash when he spoke.

'You like my touch, you hypocritical little bitch, and don't try to deny it. When I take you you're ready for me. I presume Stewart put no restrictions on sex?'

For a moment she was tempted to lie, but her pride wouldn't let her. 'No,' she said coldly.

'Then I'll take you whenever I feel like it. It seems you need a little more schooling in facing facts, Alannah.' His smile was a masterpiece of cold mockery. 'Like the fact that you enjoy my possession of you.'

'Why, you conceited ape,' she said, slowly and distinctly. 'The only way I can bear your hands and mouth on me is to close my eyes and pretend that you're David. That's why I'm——'

She never even saw his hand coming. In fact, it wasn't until some moments afterwards, when she was nursing her face in both hands, that she realised that he had hit her across the cheek, jolting her head back on her slender neck so that it was only her tight grip on the bath which had prevented her from being knocked into it.

Dimly, through the ringing in her head, she heard Nicholas swearing, ugly imprecations which seemed to come without volition. Then hard arms picked her up and as hot tears began to squeeze beneath her lashes she was carried into the bedroom and dumped on to the bed.

'Get in,' he said in a thick, low voice, 'or you'll have to bear my hands on you again while I strip you.'

For some strange reason she flinched at that, but kept her eyes tight shut until she heard the door slam. Then, like an old woman, she climbed from the bed and got into her nightgown before washing her face. Any remorse she felt at having struck so falsely at his male ego faded at the dark evidence of his blow across her cheekbone. By tomorrow the bruise would be well out, proof that he was a sadist, no better than those men who beat their wives.

Back in the bed she sighed and lay against the pillows, carefully avoiding the painful cheek. Complete understanding was supposed to be possible only with those whom one loved, yet it seemed that enmity such as theirs bred its own communion. Alannah had heard of detectives who were so attuned to the criminal mind that they could foresee each move their quarry would make. In a way she and Nick were like that.

His reaction to her impulsive insult had not

surprised her. In the split second between her words and his blow she had braced herself, fully aware of the violence she was provoking. Aware, too, that her provocation had been coldly deliberate. She had wanted to hurt him, so she had chosen to hit at that part of the male ego which is so fragile, even in a supremely self-confident man such as Nick.

Like poison her words would drip into his subconscious, eating away at him. He might not believe them; indeed, a man as experienced as he was would know that her reaction to his lovemaking had not been stimulated by fantasies, but he would never forget what she had said.

Perhaps, she thought with a savage hopefulness, perhaps he was repenting a little of that vengeful impulse which had forced her into this marriage.

On this thought she drifted off to sleep.

To be woken by a subdued hum of wheels. Ellen was pushing a trolley across the floor, her expression grim as her eyes rested on the small face against the pillows.

'Here's your dinner,' she said without preamble, adding, 'And didn't your mother tell you that if you go looking for trouble you'll get it?'

'She did, indeed,' Alannah agreed, her stomach restored to its usual state of hunger. 'Has anyone ever told Nick that?'

Incredibly Ellen's glare softened. 'I've no doubt he's learning it,' she returned drily. 'Stubborn little creature, aren't you?'

'So I've been told. I prefer to call it determined.'

'No doubt.' As Alannah sat up Ellen reached behind her and plumped up the pillows, saying, 'If you've any sense you'll give up this stupid vendetta of yours. What's done is done and for the next year or so you won't want any more turmoil and arguments. Some say that a baby is influenced by the mother's state of mind while she's carrying it. I wouldn't go that far myself, but behaving like a halfwit isn't going to do you any good.'

Alannah said with complete dislike, 'But that's what I am. If Nicholas wanted a wife who doted on him he should have courted someone who was ready to fall in love with him.' Her lip trembled and she finished on a burst of passion, 'And how dare he tell you b-before I wanted you to know!'

Ellen straightened up and stood regarding her scornfully. 'You must think all my brains are in my feet if I don't recognise the signs when I see them! Nick hasn't told me anything, you silly little idiot. Now, eat up and you'll feel better.'

'I couldn't.'

There came another of Ellen's ostentatious snorts. 'Yes, you can. I know how you feel, believe me, and it's horrible while it lasts, but it passes. Now, come on, or you'll offend me.'

'I thought the sight of me did that.'

'Did you?' The housekeeper's strong capable hands removed the lid from a bowl of chicken soup, savoury, delicately titillating. As she set the tray on Alannah's lap she said, 'Well, I've very little patience with self-pity. You must admit you've been wallowing in it since you got here.'

It should have surprised Alannah that she should be discussing her marriage so openly with this woman who had made her own feelings so blatantly obvious, but indignation drove her on.

'Self-pity?' Her voice registered disdain. Deep in the lustreless blue eyes a spark grew. She spooned some of the soup into her mouth before saying suddenly and with extreme reluctance, 'Well, so what if it is? I've had good reason, surely.'

'Possibly.' Ellen was adamant. 'But if you've any strength of character at all you'll put all that behind you. The baby is what's important now.'

'I hate this baby!' Alannah said viciously.

'I feel sorry for it. I'm sure it doesn't want to be born to a mother so immature that she'd cut off her nose to spite her face. You could have Nick eating out of your hand if you played your cards right, but will you? Oh no! Buoyed up by righteous indignation, you decide to make life as unpleasant as you can for everyone you come in contact with.'

Alannah stared at her in total bewilderment. 'Nick hates me every bit as much as I hate him.'

'Rubbish! How did that baby get there?'

Hot colour suffused the tender curve of Alannah's cheeks. 'You know as well as I do,' she was goaded into saying, 'that liking or—or love—has nothing to do with that kind of thing.'

A small grim smile touched the older woman's mouth as she surveyed the embarrassment her frankness had caused. 'I thought the young of today were supposed to be so open and candid about sex. Look at you, blushing like a schoolgirl! Of course I know the facts of life, but I know a deal more about life than the mere facts, and I know Nick too. And whatever reason he's given you for his actions I can guarantee that if he didn't want to take you to bed there'd have been no wedding.'

'I suppose I should feel honoured by his—his lust!' Alannah snapped, furious because somehow she had finished the soup and Ellen was getting much the better of this argument.

'Most do,' Ellen said nonchalantly. 'After all, it's a compliment to have a man want you. It's also some sort of base to build on.' She looked, not unsympathetically, at the bright downbent head. 'Nick doesn't tell me—or anyone—about his personal life, and I'm not so set in my ways that I can't change my mind about a person. But you'll have to pull your weight, too.'

Alannah looked up, torment showing for a moment in the darkened blue of her gaze. 'How long do they give you to recover from a death?' she asked.

'A year.'

'Well, I've ten months to go. Nick killed all my hopes and dreams when he insisted on marrying me.' Moodily she watched as Ellen removed the empty soup plate, replacing it with a singularly bland looking dinner. 'But I don't bear you any ill-will,' she said, realising that in her own odd way Ellen did care about her. Probably the fact that Nicholas's child was growing under her heart had everything to do with that, but at least it would ease things in the house not to feel that silent disapproval radiating towards her.

'Kind of you,' Ellen sniffed, not at all appeased by this placatory remark. 'I'm not the one you have to live with.'

The tender line of jaw hardened into classic belligerence. 'He made his bed,' said Alannah, not without satisfaction.

'And you'll make him suffer in it?' Ellen sounded incredulous. 'You really think you can win, don't you? Well, my lady, I've seen Nick break people before, and it's not a pleasant sight. He's every bit as tough as he looks. Best let common sense take over.'

'And just let him ride roughshod over me?' Alannah demanded passionately, forking the food on her plate with distasteful swift movements.

'It seems he's already done that.'

The glowing head nodded slyly as if Alannah was hiding a secret. 'Yes,' she said sweetly. The glance she lifted to the older woman's face was limpid and innocent.

Ellen frowned. 'Just don't expect your condition to get you any concessions,' she warned, her gaze fixed for a moment on the hot patch on Alannah's cheek. 'But you've already discovered that, haven't you?'

'Yes,' said Alannah again, turning her head away.

For a moment the housekeeper stood still, then the sound of her steps brought Alannah's head around and she watched until the door closed behind her. A long sigh trembled through her lips; she put the untasted food on to the trolley and turned on to her side, hiding her face with her upper arm.

Surprisingly enough she slept.

And slept and slept, waking up very early the next morning to a world all grey and still and cool. Continually astonished by the mildness of the climate, she lay quietly, watching through the billowing clouds of silk as the sun warmed the world to the accompaniment of a chorus of birdsong, shrill and defiant and sweetly melancholy, an instinctive recognition of light and warmth and life.

Life should be so easy, she thought cynically, warned by certain unmistakable signals that her daily ordeal was about to begin once more. Whoever heard of a mother thrush who suffered from morning sickness? Or was mated to a father thrush she loathed? No, all that birds had to worry about were minor things like where the next worm was coming from, and being eaten and the arrival of a cuckoo in the nest.

Not like Alannah Challoner, who felt such a seething resentment that it was all she could do to remain still while her husband slept the sleep of the dead beside her.

Slowly she turned her head away from the glory outside to look at him. For some reason he usually slept turned towards her, the long frame slightly curved, a possessive hand on her body. This morning was no exception. The splendid framework beneath his skin was emphasised by the absence of all expression; long thick lashes fanned down to hide the hard eyes, cast faint shadows on the dark skin of his cheeks. Freed from his habitual self-control, his mouth was no longer cruel. It had relaxed into a kind of tenderness, the full lower lip indicative of a sensuality she knew only too well.

He was beautiful, she thought dispassionately. Beautiful as a god and strong with the strength which his intelligence and his command of himself and others gave him. Had he set out to win her from David he might have succeeded, because—only now and only to herself would she admit it—he was right when he taunted her with her helpless attraction. If he had worked to overwhelm her with his sophisticated charm she might have been deceived into believing that what she felt was love.

But that was not Nicholas's plan. He wanted no adoring wife. What he needed was her physical subjugation in spite of herself, her helpless thralldom to a man she hated. Degradation of the worst sort, and he had planned it for her because only then would he be sure that her suffering would match his when he had lost Ngaire and her child.

In spite of Ellen's advice the only safety lay in her continued resistance. Her father had had a store of clichés which he trotted out on occasions. One of them had been, 'Forewarned is forearmed'. Another was 'Nothing venture, nothing win'. That was the one Nicholas had played on to bring about Holt's downfall. But the other—well, because she knew exactly what Nicholas wanted for her she would take every care not to fall into his trap.

The dark brows twitched together in a frown, giving his handsome features a forbidding air. Simultaneously the fingers on Alannah's still-narrow waist clenched.

She bit her lip, tensing, but after a moment he sighed, turning on to his back. Alannah too relaxed.

The bed was a warm nest in the cool room. Alannah's distasteful glance swept around her. How could Ngaire have chosen such an undistinguished style for a house which had immense character and distinction? They were an enigma. Poor Ngaire with her magazine tastes and this handsome ruthless cynic who had been her husband. Whatever the first Mrs Challoner had lacked in taste and creativity must have been more than compensated for by her personal characteristics. Too proud to ask, Alannah had only a few scraps of information to base any judgment on. She had been sweet, probably docile and loving, she thought with a grimace, absolutely besotted with Nick. That must be what he needed, mindless subjugation.

And because he knew he would never get it from his present wife he tried to enforce it in other ways, using the physical attraction which flamed between them as a weapon in this war of revenge on which he had embarked. Bitterly she remembered him telling her on their wedding night that things need not be like that between them.

Her open contempt of this attempt to establish some kind of accord in their marriage had been wise, for it had only been the first move in his plan to make her completely dependent on him.

How dared he! she thought furiously, prickling with anger. Subconsciously he must have a very low opinion of women if he thought she could so easily be made a fool of by the needs and desires of her body. Her hands clenched beside her, the nails cutting into the tender flesh of her palm.

A sudden movement beside her made her stiffen. Nicholas woke swiftly, in one movement, his eyes opening with none of the normal sleep-dazed wonder. Slowly his head turned and he watched her. After moments so tense she felt like screaming he yawned and said good morning in a voice a totally devoid of expression.

Alannah responded equally coolly and after a moment he asked quietly, 'How do you feel?'

'Sick.'

The bald crispness of her reply brought a frown, but he said, 'Stay where you are. I'll get you a couple of dry biscuits and a cup of tea.'

The desire to tell him not to bother trembled on her lips but Ellen's caustic observation that she'd cut off her nose to spite her face kept her silent.

He returned in a few minutes with a tray and watched with a bored expression while she ate the biscuits and drank the tea.

Then he asked coldly, 'How is your cheek?'

Incredibly she had forgotten! Colour flooded her skin as she said with stiff truthfulness, 'I can't feel it, so it must be all right.'

Something glittered in the implacable glance he bent on her. 'I'm sorry I hit you, but there was no need to announce your wrongs to the world. I won't touch you again. I wouldn't have hit you except that you offered me an intolerable insult.'

'It was you!' she spat, suffused with the familiar fury at being unable to pierce his armour of self-satisfaction. 'It was *you* who insulted *me*! You married me, treating me as if I were a doll, an empty thing with no brain or personality, no feelings, no needs! *That* is the ultimate insult! Not to have a wife who's unfaithful in her thoughts, but to be treated as if I were an android—I'll never, never forgive you for that!'

At the first bitter, desperate words he had gone pale, but when she flung the last savage sentence of denunciation at him the dark blood came beating up beneath his skin.

Surprised, buoyed by a bitter satisfaction, she hurried on, 'As for announcing my wrongs to the world—well, it's been made quite obvious to me that Ellen knows exactly why I'm here. I'd thought our marriage subject for open conversation.'

'Oh—*hell*!' The word seemed shaken from him. The flush had ebbed, leaving him pale beneath the year-round tan, and there was an odd expression in his eyes, a softening which made Alannah close her eyes swiftly against it.

The bed gave beneath his weight as he sat on its edge and took one of her hands, separating the clenched fingers.

'I have never discussed you—or our marriage—with Ellen,' he said, his voice remote. 'Are you listening, Alannah?'

'Yes.' The muttered word was barely audible. She didn't dare speak louder because his touch was doing odd things to her and it would be the worst sort of humiliation if he realised it.

'Ellen is far too astute,' he added, and his finger stroked the fine blue veins at her wrist, making her pulse leap.

Alannah took a deep breath, willing her voice to remain steady. 'Yes,' she said again, adding defiantly, 'She doesn't worry about what she says, but I didn't tell her that—that you hit me. She saw.'

'You're so right,' he said, and this time there was rueful laughter in his voice and when she opened her eyes his were fastened on the swift rise and fall of her breasts. A mocking sapient glint of amusement deepened her colour. He lifted her hand and pressed a kiss to the soft palm, watching with enjoyment as her fingers contracted at the sensuous little caress.

No! Alannah thought, so fiercely that for a moment she thought she had shouted aloud. Frantically she blurted, 'You said you weren't going to touch me again.'

That knowing humour vanished. For a moment his mouth tightened into a thin straight line then he said evenly, as though forcing himself to relax, 'My dear, can't we reach some sort of agreement. I didn't marry

you with the intention of making you as unhappy as
you obviously are. I'm sure there's enough between us
to make a reasonably good marriage.'

What a superb actor he was! Just the right note of
sincerity in his voice, just the right question in his eyes
as they searched her face. Hypocrite, *hypocrite*!

Aloud, in a smooth contained voice she said, 'I
refuse to accept you as anything other than my owner.
You used threats and force to abduct me from the
people I loved. At the time you seemed to think it was
worth it. If you've changed your mind I can't say I'm
sorry, but you needn't expect me to make the classic
response and fall in love with my ravisher.'

His lashes hid his thoughts as he let her hand fall on
to her breast. Strangely enough Alannah felt an odd
twinge of disappointment at the chiselled hauteur of
his features. It pleased her to anger him; she hated
that aloof withdrawal that didn't allow her to see if she
had drawn blood.

When Nicholas looked at her his eyes were as hard
as quartz, icy in the cold perfection of his face.

'Very well,' he said coolly, and got up from the bed
and left her.

That night he did not come home, leaving a message
with Ellen. On top of an office building he owned in
Auckland there was a penthouse. It was there that he
stayed.

As winter tightened its grip on the river Alannah
found herself alone much of the time except for the
Thurkettles. Nicholas's absences became more and
more frequent. He was often overseas. Each time he
returned he brought her back some small gift in a
taunting parody of the actions of a lover. But there
were many nights which he decided to spend in the
penthouse.

When he came home he was no longer the

dominating, cynical husband she had hated. Always courteous but distant, he treated her with careful consideration. At night they slept in the same bed, but he made no effort to touch her. At first Alannah wondered at this, only too well aware of his frequent need for the solace of a woman's body. After a while she decided that he had a mistress, and told herself that she was glad of it.

Only once did he show any anger, and that was when she tripped over a length of white drapery as she went through the door on to the terrace. It was as well that Nicholas was there. He whirled and caught her, his quick reactions saving her from a fall.

Shaken, she pulled away from his grip and sank into one of the little wrought-iron chairs, only to crack her elbow against the intricate metal. Wincing with pain, she rubbed it while stupid tears collected in her eyes.

From behind came Nicholas's voice, amused yet with a whiplash to it. 'Well, why don't you swear? That's your usual reaction to pain, isn't it?'

'I'm trying to give it up,' she retorted, casting a baleful glance at the innocent drift of silk. 'Damned thing.'

'Get rid of it.'

'What?' She stared over her shoulder at his dark silhouette against the brilliant blue of the sky. Winter though it was, the sun was warm and in the thin cotton tee-shirt his shoulders were broad, the muscles easily discernible. Elegant was the word that sprang to her mind when she thought of him, but she knew— who better?—just what strength there was in those shoulders and arms.

'Get rid of it,' he repeated, and when she still looked bewildered, he frowned impatiently. 'Redecorate the whole place, if you want to. Except for my office, of course. But at least the bedroom. I know you dislike it.'

Oh, do you? she thought, shrugging slightly. To the best of her knowledge she had never envinced any opinion about his house at all.

'I don't mind it,' she lied casually.

His voice came closer. 'You won't be surrendering any of that precious independence just by changing curtains,' he said crisply, irritation colouring his words.

'I don't want to.'

'Just as you don't want to do anything else?' He caught her by the shoulder and forced her around to face him. 'You've dived in, haven't you, and let the waters close over your head. No one would know that you're here. You've changed nothing, not even an ornament, not made a suggestion to Ellen—you don't even care enough to suggest your favourite foods.' His fingers clenched on the fine bones of her shoulder.

When she threw up her chin he let her go, drawing a short harsh breath. For a moment his eyes were bleak. 'The invisible woman,' he said tersely. 'Well, it won't work, Alannah. Like it or not, you're my wife and you're going to stay my wife. I don't care how you feel about me, so this prolonged bout of sulking isn't getting you anywhere.'

At her instinctive, startled objection he smiled narrowly, adding with silky malice, 'He couldn't have loved you very much or he would have married you out of hand. There was no stipulation about his marital status and the scholarship was worth enough to keep two with only a moderate amount of privation. I made sure he knew that.'

A kind of bitter hurt fought with pride in her countenance. Try desperately as she did to stiffen her features into a mask, she knew that he was watching her give herself away.

'And if he'd proposed I suppose you'd have given up this crazy idea,' she retorted in a thin voice.

Nicholas shrugged, 'Perhaps. To tell you the truth, I didn't anticipate anything other than what happened. I'd watched you the night before; it was easy enough to see that you were the lover, not he.'

This hurt more than anything else he had ever done to her, hurt her more than the desolation of grief after her father's death, more than the cold pitilessness of Nicholas's rape of her body. When she breathed it was like icicles in her lungs, and he knew it.

'You would have found out some time,' he said roughly and, the words releasing her from her pain, Alannah sprang to her feet and flew at him, fingers clawing for his eyes until he caught her by the wrists and forced her into a trembling, panting surrender.

'Don't you feel sorry for me!' she gasped, rigid with the savage anger his brutality had roused. 'Don't you dare—don't you *dare*——!'

His fingers tightened on her wrists as she slumped. Dimly through the roaring in her ears she heard his startled voice before she fainted.

His voice was the first thing she heard when she regained her wits. The words evaded her, but it sounded as though he was trying to justify himself, and this was so surprising that she opened her eyes.

'. . . will just have to stop!' This was Ellen, angry, each word sharp with command. 'Look at her, for heaven's sake! There's nothing of her to come and go on and she's not like—not finding pregnancy as easy as some. Fighting with her is not going to help either of you. She's as bad-tempered as you, every bit, and when you attack she'll hit right back.' The quick, hard voice softened. 'Good lord, Nick, what's come over you? I shouldn't have to give you a lecture on how to treat a woman!'

What indeed? Sickened by her own slyness in eavesdropping, Alannah tried to lever herself up on an elbow. The movement made her head swim and she sank back on to the pillows with an incoherent noise.

Both heads swung towards the bed. Ellen commanded urgently, 'Keep your head down, you little idiot!' as she came across the room.

For the first time Alannah smiled at her without reservation, a miracle of mischief which irradiated her small, wan face. 'You sound like my father.'

'And he sounds as if he was a sensible man,' Ellen told her, as she tucked an edge of the duvet in. 'Feeling better now?'

'Yes, thank you. I'm a bit thirsty.'

During this exchange Nicholas had been a silent dark figure in the background. Now, as Ellen went into the bathroom he came to stand by the side of the bed and looked down at her, that polite mask back firmly in place.

'I'm sorry,' he said quietly but without any sign of emotion.

Alannah felt old and tired and sick, her anger gone in a grey dreariness. 'Are you? But you meant what you said, didn't you?'

For a moment his gaze shifted. Then his jaw firmed and he answered, 'Yes, I stand by what I said. Which is not to say that I should have said it. That was done deliberately, to hurt you.'

'Since when have you ever regretted hurting me?' she jeered on a bitter impulse.

'Since just now,' he said, refusing to rise to her bait. His grave regard swept a face reduced to pinched plainness by nausea and the subtle slow changes of pregnancy.

Ellen was right. For some reason Alannah's healthy young body found it hard to cope with the changes her child wrought in it. The evidence was clear from the waxy colour of her skin to the shadows which enlarged her eyes and hollowed her cheeks. Although she had altered very little in size except for more voluptuous curves to her breasts and a thickening in her waistline she looked thinner and older.

'Is there nothing that can be done for this continual sickness?' Nicholas demanded wearily, running a hand through his hair.

She shook her head. 'Dr Stewart says he'd rather not prescribe anything.' Her shoulders moved slightly against the shell pink pillows. 'And I wouldn't take it if he did.'

'I see.'

Ellen came back and he left her, but that incident marked yet another turning point in their relationship. Not that his attitude to her changed; he was still courteous and considerate and rarely there. It was Alannah who found her outlook altered.

Whether his comment about David being the loved one had forced her to face something she had always carefully avoided—and even now refused to admit—it was from then on that she made a conscious effort to stop gazing back to the life which might have been and accepted that which fate had forced on to her.

As the child grew she began to relax, enjoying Ellen's acerbic, crisply sensible presence more and more. Even to the extent of giving in to her persuasion and redecorating the bedroom.

'It will,' said the housekeeper, 'give you something to do and stop you moping around.'

'Well, thank you!'

'You have only to let him know that you want him home and he'll come.'

Came that characteristic tilt of the chin as Alannah replied, 'I'm not driving him away.'

'No?' The older woman lifted disbelieving brows. 'No man is going to hang around when his presence is so obviously unwelcome.'

'He knows what to do,' Alannah said stubbornly, finding a strange bitter pleasure in discussing him.

'Oh, for heaven's sake! You're as bad as each other. Heaven help that poor child, with parents as stubborn as you two! But you might at least do something about the bedroom.'

CHAPTER SIX

So Alannah did. Surprised to discover that her own tastes in interiors were formed and very definite, she was not as surprised as the decorator Nicholas insisted on, who had been trying to persuade her into a stark modernity that repelled her by its bleakness.

'Anything else will clash with this superb house,' he said, gazing around despairingly at Ngaire's efforts.

Alannah sighed, understanding how her predecessor must have felt. He was a very trendy middle-aged man who spoke with such obvious authority that he was intimidating, but Nicholas Challoner's wife had to have the strength to stand up to anyone.

'No,' she said patiently, and by dint of repeating it, at first frequently and then as he got the idea, less so, ended up with a bedroom she liked.

While the decorators were in, Nicholas slept, on those nights when he slept at home, in a spare bedroom separate from Alannah's. And if she felt alone in the night she did not admit it even to herself.

When the room was finished he moved back with her, offering no more than a casual compliment after a quick glance around. Alannah felt as though she had been tipped into cold water. Taking herself severely to task for such stupidity, she told herself with stout courage that she liked the room, her eyes feasting on the strong deep jade green of the walls, the elegant Chinese urns and jars which picked up the colour and the bedspread on the great, low bed, the same green silk lightened with an exquisite Oriental floral design. The floor was covered in a white carpet, the furniture was white and square, at home with the modern house as well as the Oriental ambience of the room, and for emphasis there was a superb Queen Anne bureau cabinet in red lacquer with gold chinoiseries which glowed like a rare jewel in the subdued elegance of the room. It had cost so much that Alannah had dismissed it; when it turned up she had protested.

'Mr Challoner said that if you wanted it you were to have it;' the decorator told her firmly.

And that had been that. Now, running her finger up one of the domed doors, she frowned. Her husband was still as much an enigma to her as he had always been, coldly generous, yet she had no money for her own personal use; considerate in a remote impersonal fashion, he despised her, yet he had chosen her to live with him and be the mother of his children.

Now, as he showered, she chewed on her bottom lip before catching herself up guiltily and moving away from the exquisite thing to stand in the door and look out across the terrace.

Although it was winter there were still flowers blooming between the bricks, scarlet veronica, a stiff little straw daisy with flowers like suns set in gleaming silver foliage, several thymes with stray purple cones held high for the bees. Beyond them the hibiscuses still bloomed, the silken blossoms smaller than in summer but much more intense in colour. Alannah had changed Ngaire's wrought iron furniture for some made of redwood with big comfortable cushions in neutral greens and browns and instead of the intrusive sun-umbrella a pergola had been built. She was still deciding which creepers would cover it to give them shade in the summer.

Her hand stole to her waist. In the summer this one would be born, boy or girl, to lie in her arms against her heart. When she told Ellen that she hated the baby she had spoken truthfully, but yesterday she had felt a strange flutter and for the first time she had visualised the baby, not as Nick's child brutally fathered on to her, but as an individual.

And with that vision had come a kind of anguished protectiveness. Now, her fingers touching her thickened waist she grimaced and thought wearily, *God, what a mess this all is!*

'Are you not feeling well?'

The autocratic question banished her reverie. 'I never feel well,' she answered coldly, turning back into the room to face him.

His straight brows drew together. 'No, I can see that. How much longer is this—this purgatory likely to last?'

'Dr Stewart is very evasive,' she shrugged. 'All he will say is that it's most unlikely to last for the full nine months.'

'God, I hope not!'

She lifted her brows at that, delicately scathing. 'Why, Nick? Not, I know, pangs of conscience.'

'You can be quite sure of that.'

Except in the involuntary movements of sleep he had not touched her for weeks, but now he came across the room and pulled her towards him, holding her with both hands against her waist. Shaken by a frightening rush of sensation, she flinched and tried to pull away.

'No,' he said calmly, holding her in place with insulting ease. 'You're beginning to show your condition, my wife. I like it.'

'Because it proves your virility?' she retorted scornfully.

The sensual line of his lips tightened into ruthlessness. 'I needed no proof of that,' he taunted with cold deliberation. 'Ngaire was pregnant when she died, remember?'

'Why not say when I killed her?' she asked in a hard voice. 'That's what you meant, wasn't it?'

'Was it?' The pause lasted long enough for her to glance up sharply, to catch a glitter of anger deep in the green eyes. 'Of course you're right,' he mocked, lifting a hand to run it with slow menace through the curls at the nape of her neck. 'You know me so well, don't you, Alannah? You've studied me so carefully, tried to understand me, even painted this room to match my eyes.'

Her teeth met in a snap. 'It's a much darker colour than your eyes,' she flared. 'They're pale green, like ice, and every bit as cold!'

Her recklessness had its reward. Smiling, he imprisoned her head in his hands while she stared defiantly into his dark face.

'Not for you,' he said, each word a threat, lowering his head so that they made soft impressions against her mouth. 'Never for you, my sweet wife. I have only to touch you and every pulse in my body fires into life. But you know that, don't you? It gives you a perverse pleasure to know that I want you more than I've ever wanted any other woman, that you can reduce me to the level of that other poor fool who was so confident of your love that he took off to America without shackling you fast.'

'He had every reason to be confident,' she said harshly, hating him because his closeness was causing an odd weakness in her legs. 'I love him.'

He laughed and took her mouth, stretching her head back until her lips were forced open to the cruel invasion of his. Frozen, rejecting him with every cell in her body, Alannah whimpered in pain and he lifted his head, those pale eyes almost black in the flushed skin of his face.

'Let's christen this bedroom you've made,' he said sneeringly, and lifted her, carrying her across to where the enormous bed waited.

'I feel sick.' Panic made her lie as his fingers pulled the buttons of her dress free.

He smiled again and put his mouth to the swollen curve of her breast. 'I'm sure you do. You feel sick every time I touch you, don't you.'

'What do you expect?' She spoke desperately, for his mouth was moving slowly across the breasts he had released from the bra and she recognised the fierce hurtful ache which was burgeoning deep within her.

'Nothing else. Nothing else at all, my docile, amenable little wife. Just this——' His finger ran shockingly across the taut skin at her waist, probing yet caressing too. He lifted his head and looked into her baffled, angry face, his own enigmatic. 'And this,' he finished softly, and bent his head to kiss her shoulder with open mouth.

She flinched, furious because the rising excitation of her senses revealed just how out of control the situation was.

'Will—you—*stop*——!' The hot words came tumbling out as she pushed at the dark head, grabbing a handful of thick hair and yanking.

'No.'

The monosyllable was hard with purpose, as hard as the narrowed gaze that fell on her flushed face and bare shoulders and then swept down to the disarrangement he had inflicted on her. 'No,' he repeated with some satisfaction as hot colour beat up higher under her skin. 'Just lately you seem to have forgotten who you belong to, Alannah. And why you're here.'

'Forgotten?' For a moment despair showed stark in her face. 'I never forget,' she said desolately, refusing to be intimidated by the gathering darkness in his face. 'I wish I could.'

His expression was shuttered, the only live thing a spark that glowed deep in his eyes as they swept her face. Slowly, as if she hadn't spoken, his hand ran up the pale length of her thigh until it stopped just short of its destination. Tormented, she turned her head

away to droop on to the pillow while her body woke to
a vivid rushing life, every nerve end throbbing at the
deliberate sensuality of his hands and mouth.

'Just as you wish you could control this automatic
response?'

Oh, he knew her so well! For a moment she was
tempted to relax, to allow the hot tide of sensation to
overwhelm her in its forbidden brilliance. Just once,
her body urged her brain, just this once, so that I
know what it's like to sob out my desire beneath him
as he takes me to ecstasy.

But that would be surrender, a rapturous subjugation of her personality in the overwhelming masculinity
he wore as an aura about him. Once he knew that his
touch made her go wild, could make her lose every
inhibition caused by a careful, almost puritan
upbringing; once he had reduced her to mindless,
clamorous ecstasy, his triumph would be complete.

'I *can't*!' she breathed, stiffening as his index finger
slid beneath the lace that edged her briefs.

'You mean you won't.' But although the words were
a taunt his voice had thickened and he was staring at
the hollow in her throat where a pulse beat double
time, almost deafening her. His mouth came down on
it, the tip of his tongue touching the delicate skin as
though he loved its silken warmth.

Alannah winced; she had almost forgotten how
unbearable his gentleness was. It made things so much
easier for her when his hands marred her skin and his
mouth crushed hers contemptuously, but this time he
was appallingly tender, undressing her with gentle
skill, wrapping her in a net of dark sorcery as he kissed
the skin his hands exposed and told her how lovely she
was, how she tormented him with desire, the confident
strong voice oddly uncertain when he spoke.

Hurt me, she prayed, I can only take it when you
hurt me! You want to kill me, drown me in sweetness,

suffocate me with desire, make me a slave. Worse still, a slave who adores her bondage.

Only then did she appreciate the depths of the humiliation that lay in wait. But while Nicholas made love to her she was incapable of feeling anything beyond the erotic demands which his desire made. Eyes closed, because if he looked into them he would be able to judge the wildness of her reaction, she tensed to stop herself from wrapping her legs around his and pulling him down to where she ached for him—no, was on fire for him, waves of heat spreading through her body, seeking the quenching that his strength and virility could give her.

Shivers racked her. Blindly, sensually, she ran her hands from his waist to his shoulders, felt with bitter delight the sudden tensing of his muscles and explored further, the tips of her fingers delicately stroking the muscles on his arms, the smooth heated skin across his back.

He groaned her name, his mouth hot against the turgid peak of her breast, and she sighed raggedly and began to move beneath him, undulating in a way that instinct told her would further inflame him.

His hands slid to her hips; when they paused she opened tortured eyes and saw reflected in his face the agony and need that had her in its grip. And with the first hard thrust of his body the world exploded, sensation piled on sensation so that beneath her eyelids there was a sunburst of colour and she was falling, falling into its vortex, sobbing, gasping, her body racked by an ecstasy so far beyond her hidden fantasies that she thought she might die.

It was the beating of her heart which brought her back to her senses. It thumped, in her breast, in her ears, so heavily that she could feel it shaking her body.

Slowly, so slowly that there was no pinpointing the exact moment when it happened, the sleek contentment

invoked by his lovemaking was replaced by melancholy, deep and dark and tinged with shock. So that
was it, that was the heart of the mystery. Millions of
words had been written in an effort to describe it, the
indescribable, but Alannah had never read of this
intensity of *tristesse* which followed the most shattering
experience of her life.

Shattered too were her ideals. Always she had
divined that Nicholas had the power to drive her out of
her mind. If she was candid she must admit that that
had been one of the reasons for hating him,
instinctively and at first sight. For if she loved David
what sort of woman was she to respond so ardently to
the sexual promise of another man? As she had. Her
sixteen-year-old self had recognised the tug of
attraction, recognised it and been fascinated and
repelled by it.

Only too readily her brain supplied words to describe
her sort of woman, harsh, ugly words which
condemned and excoriated.

The muscles beneath the silken skin of her throat
moved. Jerkily she twisted away from him to hide the
tears which were hot beneath her lashes. As if her
movement was a signal Nicholas lifted his head,
ordering harshly:

'Look at me.'

Her only reply was to bury her face into the pillow,
but one hand caught her chin and forced her around.

'So now we know,' he said softly.

The cynical appraisal in his voice dragged her lashes
upward. His face was so close that it was blurred, but
only too clearly could she discern the irony that
twisted his mouth.

Well, of course he despised her. The wild abandon
of her response could do nothing but increase the
contempt which was his main feeling for her. But if he
dared to taunt her she would kill him, she vowed.

Perhaps he noticed the defiant little movement of her chin, perhaps the gloss of dampness in her eyes warned him of her lack of self-command. Whatever, he lifted himself from her, pulling the coverlet over her sweat-soaked body.

'You'd better have a shower,' he said coolly. 'I'll get Ellen to bring your dinner in on a tray.'

Lost in the folds of the dramatic dark jade and cream spread she had chosen with such care, Alannah closed her eyes again, careless of anything but her humiliation.

After that he left her strictly alone so that she lay beside him at nights and wondered sickly why he had forced that tumultuous ravishment. To prove that she was no better than the other women who had found a dangerous ecstasy in his arms?

It seemed that must be the reason. And Alannah's resolution not to succumb hardened into almost an obsession. Now that she knew how perilous the least weakening could be there must never be another, for Nicholas knew too, and no doubt he planned to use her body's weakness to reduce her to a shamed subservience.

Well, he would find out! And in the cool nights her chin would lift in unseen defiance while the sound of his breathing blended with the soft noise of the waves at the foot of the cliff.

Not that the estuary suffered very big waves, even in winter. There were days when rain and wind and sea whipped the surface of the water up into a grey turbulence, but more days when the sun laughed over the landscape, enchanting it.

'I can't believe it!' Alannah felt that she would never stop saying it. She said it when she picked kiwi-fruit from the vine, warm and ripe and furry, and ate as many as she liked, she said it when on the shortest day Hugh brought in great bunches of camellias and sweet-smelling jonquils for her to arrange.

The first mandarin, sweet and easily peeled, brought forth the same reaction, and because fruit was one of the few foods which she could eat easily she said it when Hugh showed her tamarillos, glowing ruby-red eggs beneath their enormous leaves, and guavas and goldfruit, enormous citrus fruit which Ellen squeezed for juice at breakfast.

Then came irises, pale blue and one so dark it was a kind of electric ultramarine and lemon-scented daphne, the bunches of pink flowers like small clusters of stars so low to the ground. And when the native manuka bloomed in white clouds beside the road its more exotic cousins lit up corners of the garden with their little crinkly flowers in all the shades of pink and red, some single, some as ruffled as a ballerina's tutu.

'You don't have a winter!' Alannah told Ellen severely.

'You wait till next year, my girl. You'll be acclimatised by then and you'll be pulling on jerseys and complaining about the cold.'

Alannah grinned. 'You don't even have frosts!'

'Not down by the sea we don't, but they have them farther inland.'

'*Never* any snow.'

Ellen smiled dryly. 'It did snow in Auckland some years ago. For five minutes. And judging by the fuss you'd have thought another ice age was on the way!' Her shrewd eyes ran over Alannah's rapidly enlarging shape. 'You're looking better.'

Nicholas had been away for a week, a business trip to San Francisco, and during that time the constant nausea had relaxed its grip on Alannah. Perhaps it was the release from the constant tension engendered by his cool detachment.

'I feel better,' she admitted.

Over the months Ellen's attitude had warmed appreciably, but Alannah still felt as though she was guarded by a schoolmistress with a fierce tongue who made no exceptions! So Alannah treated her with a polite reserve and relaxed only with the silent Hugh.

But Hugh had already left to pick Nicholas up from the evening plane, and the coils of tension in Alannah's stomach were tightening. For some reason she no longer had the desire to resist him. As her pregnancy advanced it seemed to slow her down, not only physically but emotionally. As placid as a gestating cow, she thought wryly, no tantrums, no sly jibes, no digs. Nick's reasons were clear enough. No doubt he wanted his child to have the best start in life possible, and a mother constantly simmering with fury was hardly that!

The telephone's insistent ring disturbed her thoughts. Ellen answered it and after a moment came on to the wide atrium where Alannah lay curled up in the sun between great pots of begonias and impatiens, and announced:

'That was Nick.'

'Oh?' Perhaps he wasn't coming home. A nameless emotion deepened Alannah's voice. 'What did he want?'

'He's bringing visitors home—the Sterlings, Caroline and Ralph. Father and daughter.'

Alannah blinked her astonishment then got up and followed Ellen into one of the guest rooms.

'Like all men,' Ellen said tersely, pulling the curtains straight, 'he expects everything to be miraculously ready. Still, he's usually very good about letting me know. *No!*' as Alannah set off towards the bathroom, 'I'll do that! You go and pick flowers.'

'This,' Alannah told the bulge of her stomach severely ten minutes later as she cut a branch of crab-apple blossom and put it in the trug, 'this is what you've reduced me to, infant. A mere picker of flowers!'

But the blossom looked superb in the room she had allotted to Caroline Sterling. For her father there was a masculine arrangement of leaves and gladioli and a small bowl of cottage pinks to scent the air with their clove perfume.

'You have the touch,' Ellen commented.

Colour warmed Alannah's cheeks. Ellen was so sparing of her compliments that each new one was like a jewel. It emboldened her to ask, 'Have the Sterlings ever been here before?'

'Oh yes. Often.'

'What are they like?'

Ellen shrugged, shooting her a swift, shrewd look. 'Pleasant enough. Mr Sterling does business with Nick. She'd have liked to be the second Mrs Challoner.'

'Oh.' For a moment Alannah found herself struggling with a strange new complex of emotions, horrified to realise that the uppermost was one of outrage! It frightened her to discover that although she could never love her husband she had developed a kind of possessiveness about him.

'I suppose she's stunningly beautiful,' she said gloomily, grabbing for dignity.

Ellen smiled rather sardonically. 'Well, yes.'

'It figures.'

'What do you want for breakfast tomorrow morning?'

Which meant the time for confidences was over. Alannah discussed the menu for a few minutes, went through every room in a last-minute check, moved a superb Chinese vase of grey-green porcelain six inches towards the centre of its table in the sitting room, then made determinedly back to the bedroom.

As always the room brought a lift to her heart, but she had time only to cast a sparkling look around before heading for the dressing room.

Very few of the clothes she had brought with her fitted now, but the last time she had gone to Auckland she had bought a dress, a pretty thing in startling acid greens which somehow harmonised with the colour of her hair. Not that her hair was in good trim. Pulling a fierce face at her reflection, she went into the shower to wash it, and was seated on the bed in her dressing-gown blow-drying it when her husband touched her shoulder.

'Oh!' she exclaimed as the frenetic buzz of the dryer faded. 'Oh, you're early!'

He shrugged. 'Half an hour or so. I'm sorry if we threw your plans into disarray.'

The cool dismissive tone ruffled her, but she knew better now than to react to it.

'I'm so sorry I wasn't ready to greet your guests,' she said, groaning as the baby objected to her change of position by kicking vigorously. A fugitive dimple just below her mouth gave her a mischievous childlike air. 'You know, sometimes I think I'm going to be the first woman in the world to give birth to an octopus!'

Nicholas smiled, but there was no amusement in it. Rebuffed, Alannah shrugged slightly as she went across the room. The decision to treat him as a stranger had been hers, she was more than content with his absences and his cool aloofness, the way he never touched her, the fact that when he looked at her the blazing brilliance in his eyes had been replaced by a remote politeness—why then should she be chilled by his refusal to meet this first friendly advance she had made to him?

Yet she did, and the strange feeling of alienation continued even after she had pulled on the new dress and made up her face. The horrible nausea of the early months had decreased, but her stomach was still easily upset and this showed in her face. Pregnancy made many women bloom; it seemed appropriate to her that it should drain the natural colour from her cheeks and emphasise her eyes with shadows which made her look at once older and very tired. Even made up she was no competition for anyone, let alone a beautiful Caroline Sterling who had hoped to be Nick's second wife.

For the first time in her life she wished that she had Trina's height and striking good looks, instead of the ordinary little face and figure reflected in the mirror. Even the blue of her eyes, her best features, had faded.

'Ready?'

Nicholas's voice in the doorway turned her head. For a moment she thought he had seen that intent, searching scrutiny she had given herself, but if he had he gave no sign of it.

'Yes.'

The unsparing survey of his eyes brought her head up but he said merely, 'That dress suits you. You need—wait a moment.'

What she needed were earrings, dark emeralds in a cabochon cut, the smooth glowing ovals almost Gothic in appearance. Alannah stared at them, then lifted her eyes to his.

'They're very lovely,' she said. 'Where—whose are they?'

Anger compressed his lips. 'Yours,' he said briefly. And when she made no effort to put them on he added brutally, 'They were not Ngaire's, if that's what you mean. She liked sapphires and pearls; she would have thought these barbaric.'

Almost she flinched. Her fingers trembled as she slid the gems on to her lobes. He had told her nothing about the jewellery, but some instinct warned her to ask no more, for he was keeping a tight leash on his temper, barely containing it.

Why? she thought, but there was no answer.

When she turned away from the mirror Nicholas

was once more in control, the sophisticated, urbane mask firmly in place.

Caroline Sterling was inordinately beautiful. It was quite unfair for one woman to have so much, Alannah thought dispassionately as she said all the right things to her guest. Tall, yet of a height to bring out a man's protective instincts, with a body too curvaceous for modelling but not so ripe that a man who liked slender women would be put off, a skin like smooth matt satin, pale gold beneath hair exquisitely silver-blonde— probably artificial, but so natural that one couldn't be sure—and that face! Superb bone structure emphasised by large hazel eyes and a melting, ripe mouth which made every word she spoke a sensuous experience. As beautiful in her way as Nick was in his, both with the vitality of perfect health.

Alannah felt old and weary and dowdy, even after Caroline's eyes had rested on the emeralds with a hastily concealed covetousness.

This sneaking sense of inferiority was hateful; it was totally new to her. All her life she had known that Trina was the prettier of the two and there had been other girls with real claims to beauty whom she had liked or not, but never had she felt like this. It was Nick's fault, impregnating her, forcing her to carry his child so that all the cosmetics in the world could not give her skin that glow of health.

Unconsciously her hand sought her waist where the child lay quiescent now. It was a revealing little gesture, had she known it.

Caroline Sterling asked sweetly, 'When is the baby due, Mrs Challoner?'

'Call me Alannah,' she responded automatically, at the same time as Nick spoke.

'In the summer,' he told her with an aloof authority.

Caroline lifted her brows. 'So soon? It's unusual

nowadays for people to start a family quite so quickly, isn't it?'

'I'm thirty,' Nick said smoothly, smiling down at Alannah while his eyes commanded her backing.

'But Alannah is so young!' protested Caroline, smiling too to show that she was speaking lightly while those gold eyes were every bit as cold as Nick's as they assessed her hostess. Young, they said scornfully, and totally insignificant.

Mr Sterling moved a little uncomfortably. 'My dear——' he began just as Alannah spoke.

'I suppose nineteen seems young to you,' she said sweetly, burning her boats, 'but my mother was only eighteen when I was born, and it's been fun having a mother like a big sister.'

The exquisite countenance tightened for a moment, then eased into a smile as sweet as syrup.

'Well, I suppose it's your decision,' she murmured, flirting her lashes at Nick as she went on playfully, 'Although if I know your husband at all I'll bet he was the one who made it. Masterful is exactly the right word for you isn't it, Nick? Strong and masterful as a warrior prince!'

Most men would have blinked or been embarrassed by this rather fulsome compliment delivered in a voice heavy with innuendo, but you had to hand it to Nicholas. He lifted one eyebrow, smiled with a nice blend of irony and affection and said with cool deliberation, 'Which is just a different way of calling me dictatorial, I'm afraid. And as Alannah is busy working her way through the Thesaurus, beginning with "arrogant", she doesn't need any help from you, Caroline.'

'Oh?' Caroline was taken aback and more than a little inquisitive, but either good manners or a certain respect for Nicholas's temper kept her silent.

And Nicholas grinned, allowing his eyes to roam over his wife's face as he said on a meaning note,

'Don't let that sweet, docile little face delude you. Alannah has the sort of character which goes with that glorious hair—up like a bush-fire, with the tongue of a virago to match. In ten years' time, when she's learned some control, she'll have strong men trembling in their shoes!'

Of course he was taunting her, that teasing, laughing note in the deep voice just a cover for his real emotions, but it sounded as though they enjoyed the kind of tempestuous, passionate relationship which could be heaven or hell. And that for them it was mostly heaven.

Colour touched Alannah's cheeks; she looked sideways up at him from beneath her lashes and said mockingly, 'Nick, I'm sure Mr Sterling and Caroline aren't interested in our battles—however satisfying we find them.'

It was Mr Sterling who answered, his handsome florid face relaxing into joviality. 'Sounds to me as if you've met your match, Nick,' he said, chuckling. 'Like Katharina and Petruchio in *The Taming of the Shrew*, eh?'

'Hardly.' Caroline was scornful and allowed it to show. 'Unless Nick has schemes for turning Alannah into a downtrodden, tractable creature like poor Katharina at the end of the play.' Her bright, knowing eyes quizzed him. 'Is that it, Nick? You've decided to try your hand at taming a shrew yourself?'

Alannah's skin prickled with dislike, but she said nothing, warned by the glitter in Nicholas's glance that she had better watch her step. After all, her reference to Caroline's age had brought this upon her; she had known from the first moment she had set eyes on the older woman that Caroline had not come prepared to like Nick's wife, but she should not have allowed her own peculiar antagonism to provoke her into bitchy comments.

Hoping that her little start of surprise when he took her hand would go unnoticed, she watched as he raised it to his mouth and kissed the wrist with such grace that she found herself wondering if there was any Mediterranean blood in him.

Still holding her hand, he said lightly, 'And risk boring myself to tears with a compliant, deferential wife? You know me better than that, Caro.'

There was a faint note of warning in his voice. Caroline caught it and smiled to cover up some complicated emotion.

'Certainly it doesn't sound like you,' she said easily, seeming suddenly much more confident. 'How sensible of you not to change things in here, Alannah. The whole house is so distinguished, so—so balanced and ordered.' She laughed a little self-consciously. 'Like its owner, austere, formal, yet with immense charisma. And you can laugh at me if you like, Nick, but you know that you and the house are perfect for each other.'

So she had never seen Ngaire's bedroom. For some reason this thought gave Alannah a small glow of satisfaction as Nick made some teasing comment. The illogical emotion lasted while they finished their drinks and then moved into the dining room.

It was a pleasant enough meal. Had the guests been any others Alannah could even have enjoyed herself. She hadn't realised how very cut off she had been from even ordinary social occasions. As well as keeping her short of money Nicholas had imprisoned her in this beautiful house of his. Caroline called him austere and formal—did she know of the grinding lust for revenge beneath that charismatic surface, the cruelty and the remorseless patience? For three years he had waited, spinning a web of ruin about the Finderne family so that Alannah would be forced to provide him with the child he wanted so desperately.

Caroline had spoken of order, of balance. Was that how he saw it, a balancing of scales, a life for the life she had taken, a child for the one her carelessness had killed? Surely the yearning for order could not become so extreme a passion. At first she had thought his object had been straight revenge, the need to inflict a similar hurt to the one she had unwittingly dealt him, but that was too simplistic a reason.

Her lashes lifted as she glanced down the gleaming length of the table to where he sat, smiling at something Caroline had said, the disturbing classic beauty of his features failing entirely to hide the complete self-sufficiency of the man. Caroline held her glass out, pouting prettily as he poured wine into it.

Unaware of her absorbed expression, Alannah watched the movements of his hands. It seemed incredible—it *was* incredible—to realise that those hands had touched her, caressed her slender body with exquisite precision and an inborn knowledge of what they were doing. How could two people be as close as they were and so distant? This man who possessed her, this complex, subtle man, was a complete stranger, alien, unknown.

For a moment fear swamped her, a strange cold emotion. From a distance she heard Ralph Sterling's concerned voice.

Swallowing, she closed her eyes, then managed to force a smile as she turned her head his way.

'I'm sorry,' she said quietly, 'I was daydreaming.'

He looked relieved and knowing, the handsome ruddy face a little more flushed with food and wine. 'And I know what about! I haven't forgotten what it's like being newly married!'

She smiled politely, wishing she had been more circumspect in the direction of her gaze.

'You look rather pale.' Caroline's voice grated, her words unwelcome. 'Dad, have you frightened her?'

He made a laughing disclaimer and Nicholas said, 'Alannah?'

It could have been a query about the state of her wine-glass, but he was asking how she felt. Sudden anger spurted into her veins. Lifting her head, she said lightly, 'No wine for me, thank you, Nick.'

The dark haughtily-poised head inclined, but after that she felt his thoughtful regard on her face more frequently, and when he and Mr Sterling made to go into the office he asked with seeming solicitude, 'Do you want to go to bed now? I'm sure Caroline will understand if you do.'

'Of course.' Caroline's magnificent face expressed only a rather patronising pity. 'Honestly, Alannah, I'll be perfectly happy watching television in front of the fire.'

It was tempting, but Rose's training was too ingrained.

'No, I feel fine,' Alannah replied lightly, and smiled up at Nick. 'You mustn't treat me like an invalid, you know. Dr Stewart says that's very bad policy!'

He said something mildly amusing and left them. And, as she had known would happen, immediately the men had left the room Caroline gave up any pretence.

'You don't have to entertain me,' she said, settling back into her chair. 'I'm quite good at keeping myself occupied. And I know the house very well, so you needn't stay up if you're tired. Nick and I are such old friends that I'm sure he doesn't really consider me a guest here.'

'I'm sure he doesn't.' Well, it was the only polite rejoinder, but it cost her an effort to make it.

Caroline looked around with bright, greedy eyes at the magnificent Persian carpet on the floor, the rows of books, then came to rest on a bronze Chinese incense burner in the shape of a deer.

'That's Sung dynasty,' she said abruptly.

Alannah's hair shimmered like living silk in the glow of the fire as she nodded. 'Yes, I know.'

'Nick told me it represents the dwarf deer that lived in the Emperor's miniature gardens.'

The statement was a challenge. Alannah settled back into the glove-soft leather of her chair, her drooping lashes hiding her thoughts.

'Fascinating,' she said politely.

Caroline flung her a condescending glance. 'Of course Nick has superb taste. He wanted Ngaire to decorate and furnish it, but she couldn't see past chintz and ruffled curtains, so he got in a decorator and told him exactly what he wanted. And being Nick, what he wanted was what he got.' She curled her magnificent lip. 'Ngaire just went along with everything. She thought the sun shone out of Nick.'

There wasn't really an answer to that, so Alannah merely said, 'Yes,' in a courteous voice and suggested turning the television on. She definitely didn't want to hear any more confidences about the woman whose death she had caused. At least it didn't seem that the Sterlings knew of that.

'No, I'm not that interested in the box,' Caroline told her. 'Ngaire was my cousin.'

'Oh!' Surprise coloured Alannah's soft tones. 'I didn't realise that.'

'No, I could see that. We see a lot of Nick, Dad and I.' The splendid column of white throat was arched as a small reminiscent smile played about the full mouth. 'He and I have a lot in common. He was devoted to Ngaire, of course, but I've often thought it was because she absolutely worshipped him. Men tend to love the women who love them, don't they, and Ngaire was a stunning blonde and sweetly helpless with it.'

Dark lashes lifted as her gaze swept Alannah's smooth abstracted countenance. After a short pause which might have invited a comment she said maliciously, 'That's why you're such a surprise. You look far from helpless and I'm sure you're far too sensible to hanker after beauty.'

'You're so right,' Alannah murmured, and there was no one to tell Caroline that the sardonic appreciation in the younger woman's voice was because she was so wrong. Against Nick's particular brand of ruthlessness Alannah was completely helpless. And for some strange reason at this moment she would have given much to be a raving beauty.

'Where did you meet Nick?' Caroline went on.

Alannah moved restlessly but answered with grave composure, 'My father and he had business dealings together.'

'I see.' Delicate scorn in the clear voice. 'Who is your father?'

A spark lit the cool blue depths of Alannah's eyes. 'Holman Finderne. Most people knew him as Holt.'

'Oh, I know the name, of course. Hasn't Nick just taken over the firm in Christchurch?'

Alannah nodded. 'Yes. Dad died last year.'

'So it was a merger in several ways. You must miss your family.'

'I do,' Alannah said simply, realising how much she longed for the tall, solemn Trina, pretty, silly Rose, and David—oh, *David*! her sore heart cried.

'Homesickness is hell, isn't it?' But Caroline didn't sound in the least sympathetic and the glance that rested on Alannah's face was bright and sharp. 'Still, being Nick's wife must be quite some compensation. Apart from the man, who is completely devastating, there's this fabulous house and all that lovely loot. A pity you don't feel well enough to entertain or be entertained, but I suppose that can wait until after the baby has come. When she was pregnant Ngaire was absolutely bursting with good health, poor darling.'

Good for Ngaire, Alannah thought sourly. Aloud she remarked, 'It takes different people different ways. Ellen tells me that a lousy pregnancy often means an easy birth and a good baby. I hope she's right.'

'Yes.' Patently Caroline wasn't interested in Ellen's prognostications. 'Well, she should know, she's had half a dozen or so kids, I believe. How long is this sickness going to last?'

Alannah shrugged, impatient and irritated. 'I wish I knew.'

'Oh, well, I suppose you wouldn't want to go to a ball anyway, however well you felt.' The hazel eyes ran disparagingly down to rest on Alannah's waist. 'You couldn't dance, could you, and it would be boring to be stuck on the sidelines all evening.'

'Almost certainly,' said Alannah at her driest, her great eyes suddenly alert and interested. 'What ball are we talking about?'

'Oh, it's a charity ball, Nick's favourite. We always make up a party and go and as Nick is the president he has to be there, of course. It's in three weeks' time in Auckland. An absolutely fabulous night out.' She leaned forward, revealing the voluptuous swell of her breasts and an area of smooth tanned shoulder. 'It's the social event of the year. We have dinner first and then we go on to the ball and usually end up somewhere for breakfast. Marvellous!'

'It sounds it.' Alannah smiled, thinking that Caroline really was too glossy, more like the projection of a man's fantasy than a real woman.

Why hadn't Nick married her? She was clearly more than willing; every time she spoke his name a husky note in her voice revealed how strongly she was affected by him. Alannah suddenly shivered, cold in the warm, beautiful room. Was it because he didn't have to pretend with Alannah, or be bothered with her? Caroline would be a demanding wife, expecting far more from him than the impersonal passion and cool politeness which made up his attitude to his wife.

As if satisfied by the reaction she had exacted, Caroline leaned back in her chair, sleek, almost smug, half closing her eyes as she spoke.

'Never mind,' she said dulcetly, 'there's always next year. Unless you're pregnant again, of course. Nick is certainly making up for lost time, isn't he? I sometimes think it was the baby he was most grieved at losing, poor sweet. He and Ngaire tried for three years, you know. She was getting pretty desperate.' Her laughter trilled forth, edged with malice. 'Now we know who was the one lacking, don't we? *Not* Nick!'

'No, indeed.' Repressing a shudder at the feverish, avid envy in the other woman's bold glance, Alannah felt a little sick. So that was why he had been so angry when she had twitted him with his virility. Poor Ngaire, to have waited so long and then to die. God, would she never be able to rid herself of the remorse, the anguish that still held her prisoner? Nick thought that his threats had driven her into this bondage, but she knew now that behind his words there was Ngaire's reproachful ghost; that was why she was here with this elegantly malicious woman, listening to her trying to poison her marriage.

If she only knew!

'I say, are you all right?' Caroline sounded perturbed and annoyed. 'You've gone a funny colour. Do you want a drink of water or something? Brandy?'

Unable to repress a shudder, for as well as coffee she was now unable to cope with alcohol, Alannah shook her head.

'No, it will pass. It always does.'

'Well, I think you should go to bed. You look as though you're going to pass out. Can I help you? Or get Ellen?'

The last thing she wanted was Caroline's help.

'No,' she said wearily, 'I'll be fine.'

'Oh, good. I'd get Nick, but he and Daddy are talking business.' As Alannah hesitated Caroline said impatiently, 'Look, don't think you have to be a good hostess. Ellen will have left coffee ready for the men; I'll take it in in a few minutes and then I'll go to bed too. If I know them they'll be up until all hours.'

Apparently Caroline had been well trained too. Business was sacred. As she made her way down the corridor a sudden spark of defiance made Alannah knock on the office door.

Nick's voice called something and she went in, to meet a frown that deepened as he saw her. He looked as cool and elegant as ever, leaning against the edge of his desk with a paper in his hand, long legs supporting him—as great a contrast as one could imagine to the man with him. In spite of his excellent tailor Ralph Sterling looked big and bulky, dwarfing the fireplace as he stood by it, a cigar in one hand, a glass of something in the other into which he too was frowning.

'Alannah?' Nick said swiftly as he got to his feet and came towards her.

She nodded at him and smiled warmly at the other man. 'Sorry to interrupt, but I'll have to go to bed,' she said quietly. 'Caroline very kindly said she'll bring the coffee in for you later. I'm so sorry, Mr Sterling.'

His broad, handsome features had relaxed. 'Don't worry about it, my dear. When she was pregnant my wife used to go to bed at eight o'clock every night!'

She smiled, as he meant her to, and turned as Nicholas slid an arm around her waist.

'Give me five minutes, Ralph,' he said over his shoulder.

'Certainly. Goodnight, Alannah.'

'Goodnight, Mr Sterling.'

Once outside the door she protested softly, 'I'm quite capable of getting there myself, you know.'

'Yes, even if you have to crawl.' His voice was harsh but he kept his arm around her. 'And I'm well aware that you'd rather crawl than have me help you.'

She shrugged, holding herself very upright. 'I'm tired, nothing else.'

'Don't be an idiot,' he said wearily. 'I only have to look at you to see how much this is taking out of you. Stop trying to crack so hardy.'

'Worried about the baby?'

His fingers at her waist tightened cruelly, then relaxed. 'What else?' he said with smooth logic. 'However, Stewart assures me that in spite of the fact that you look like death warmed up you're actually quite fit.'

'And, of course, the baby will be fine,' she observed dulcetly. 'Like a parasite, it grows and flourishes.'

He opened the door with a mock-bow. 'Is that how you think of it?'

The temptation to lie was almost overwhelming, but she had vowed never to lie to him. 'No,' she said slowly. 'Not since it started moving.'

'Instinct overrides everything.' He spoke with a wry note that brought her head up sharply. For a long moment her eyes searched his face, met the cool hooded remoteness of his, and then she sighed.

'Oh, it does indeed. Goodnight.'

CHAPTER SEVEN

CAROLINE had been right. It was two o'clock before
Nicholas came to bed, and then he did not go straight
to sleep but lay on his back, hands clasped behind his
head as he stared at the ceiling.

Kept awake by the unwelcome activity of the child
they had made, Alannah tried to lie still, but after
what seemed an hour but was probably only five
minutes, she swung her legs on to the floor and made
her way to the bathroom.

Once up she felt wide awake, too alert to go back
and lie beside a wakeful husband. In spite of the
intimacies they had shared she was still shy of him.
During the day she hid this beneath the assurance of
her manner, but in the closeness of the big bed her
diffidence made her selfconscious, acutely aware of
every movement he made, the warmth that seeped
from his body, the small sounds of his breathing. He
knew, too; she could see the knowledge in his eyes
when she avoided any positions which might lead to a
casual meeting of limbs. Her prickly shyness gave him
a caustic pleasure. He was not in the least embarrassed
by her presence, moving about their suite as if he were
alone, often splendidly naked.

She should be accustomed to his presence, but it
was this resistance which drove her over to the
window now, shivering slightly as she watched clouds
move majestically across the sky. It was a fine night lit
by a waning moon, which made the waters of the
estuary a pale sheet against the darker hills. Far out to
sea a lighthouse sent its protective sweep across the
waters in a regular pattern. Alannah counted it,

higgledy-piggledy one, higgledy-piggledy two ...
watching with eyes unconsciously wistful. From
somewhere up on the hill one of the cows made a
muted sound, a quiet reassurance to its calf, probably.
The river was empty of its abundant life, dreaming its
slow quiet dreams of the tide's inexorable progress.
There was no light from any of the farmhouses on the
opposite side.

'You'll get cold.'

Nick's voice made her shiver and turn back into the
room. Obeying the unspoken command, she walked
back, steeling herself to get under the blankets.

'It's too cold to wander around without a dressing
gown,' he said roughly, touching her shoulder. 'Stupid
girl.'

Indeed, like a traitor within, a fit of shivering racked
her. She heard the sibilant hiss of an imprecation, then
she was drawn with rather more force than necessary
against his hard, warm body.

'If you will persist in these childish attempts to
escape my presence you'll have to take the conse-
quences,' he said, ignoring the quick stiffening of her
body. 'Lie still.'

She must have been tireder than she thought, for
even as she began to protest a yawn caught her, and by
the time it was over she was too comfortably encircled
by his body to carry on with her protest. His breath
stirred the top hairs on her head, she could feel the
hard wall of his chest behind her shoulders, his legs
kept hers warm. One hand lay on the bulge of her
abdomen, and for once his child made no protest.

'Goodnight,' he murmured quietly.

Alannah yawned again, shaken by a weariness she
no longer resisted.

Caroline Sterling and her father stayed that day and
the next night, not leaving until after lunch. Alannah

was glad to see them go. Caroline had spent much of the time they were together making insinuating little remarks until Alannah was left in no doubt just how close the relationship between her and Nick had been.

Still was, for all that Alannah knew; Caroline didn't tell her that! And, tormented by this new and niggling sense of ownership which had sprung up overnight, Alannah found that the image of Nick in the beautiful Caroline's bed angered her.

Angered her even more than the smug possessiveness in the other woman's eyes whenever they rested on her host, though that was infuriating too. At least Nick didn't respond to the open invitation of Caroline's manner. He treated her with a bland courtesy which could have hidden anything.

Life seemed to slow after that weekend. Confined to the easier walks about the farm, Alannah found that her increasing size hindered her mobility more and more. She allowed herself to be bullied by Ellen into making clothes for the new baby—such tiny little garments!—although she kept them hidden from Nick's sarcastic gaze.

And wearing a bathing suit Ellen had produced for her, she swam a lot in the pool, lazily content to bask in the heated water until Ellen told her sternly that exercise was the object of it all. Grumbling, she did her lengths each day, surprised and rather pleased as the number increased weekly.

The nausea faded, although she still had to be careful of what she ate, and her looks didn't improve. Nick was at home for much of the time, still remote and cool towards her.

But when he spoke of staying in Auckland one weekend she lifted her head, suddenly angry.

'Because of this ball?'

His eyebrows climbed. 'As it happens, yes. Who—oh, Caroline, of course.'

'Of course.' Oh, why did she have to snap like that? Now he would twit her with jealousy, and *she was not* jealous. Envious, perhaps. It was so long since she had had any fun.

But although he was watching her closely there were no snide comments forthcoming.

Instead he said quietly, 'I'm obliged to be there, I'm afraid.'

'Of course,' she repeated, and this time the waspish note was so blatant that she expected instant retribution. Indeed, she peeped through her lashes at him, waiting. Instead she saw an expression of immense weariness pass over his face. For a moment she was gripped by a strange emotion, one that she had never experienced before. It hurt, and she asked impulsively,

'Are things not going well?' At his astonished glance she muttered, 'You look tired.'

'Do I?' He seemed amused by this. 'So you do look at me occasionally!'

'I can't avoid it.'

He grinned at her spirited retort and came around to stand behind her, pulling her head back by the curls that clustered at the nape of her neck. Seen upside down his face was intriguingly introverted, the harshly beautiful lines forming a pattern at once familiar and strange.

'That's more like you,' he said, tracing the line of her brow with a gentle finger. The soft caressing touch closed her eyes, then moved down the straight nose to rest on the warm firmness of her lips.

'What do you mean?' she asked.

'When you talk it feels like kisses against my skin.' He ran the finger down the proud arch of her throat, rested it for a moment in the hollow and then released her to slide both hands to the full tenderness of her breasts.

It was so long since he had touched her in any but the most impersonal way that Alannah was terrified by the wave of hot excitement that flooded her, causing turmoil in the deepest centres of her body.

'Don't!' she protested, her voice high and shrill with shock.

Nicholas's head was bent forward so that he spoke into her ear, causing more erotic sentations. 'You don't really mean that. Would you like me to stay here this weekend?'

By now her dismay at her weakness overrode the delicious sensations his hands roused.

'No!' she spat. 'I'd rather you spent every weekend in Auckland!'

His hands tightened painfully. Then his teeth met on the lobe of her ear, painfully exciting, and she was free.

'I'm afraid that would cause even more comment,' he said calmly, as though the last few minutes hadn't occurred. 'My friends are convinced that I'm so insanely jealous of you that I refuse to let you out.'

'They're going to be disappointed when they meet me,' she retorted, adding with a pseudo-sweetness which cost her a considerable amount of effort, 'I've no doubt Caroline is doing her best to convince everyone that the gossip is widely off the mark.'

'She is,' he said, the deep voice more than a little bored, 'but although exquisitely beautiful and very sexy, Caroline isn't terribly clever. She finds it astonishing that all of our acquaintances should listen to her description of you and remain convinced that I must adore the ground you walk on. Why else would I marry you?'

'Certainly not for my looks,' she shot back. 'Or my personality. But sooner or later someone will find out why, Nick. What will you do then? I'm sure it won't do your image any good. Most people, even hardheaded businessmen, would find your plan a little too ruthless to swallow.' She turned, gave him a dazzling false smile. 'Normal people don't marry people they loathe just for revenge. Aren't you afraid that your friends will start looking sideways at you?'

'Not in the least,' he retorted blandly. 'If—when it becomes general knowledge that you caused Ngaire's death I'll let it be known also that after seeing you then I was so impressed that I didn't lose touch.' He smiled, cold dislike hardening his features into an icy mask. 'When we met again after your year away we fell instantly in love. A romantic little story, don't you think? With the added advantage of being almost true.'

'I'm quite sure no one who knows you will believe such a—such a pack of claptrap,' she said contemptuously.

'Are you? But people are surprisingly easy to fool. Look at your mother. She's completely convinced that you and I are devoted to each other.'

Alannah turned away from the cold sarcasm of his gaze, hating him, hating herself for precipitating this scene. She no longer had the stamina for them. It seemed incredible that at the beginning of their marriage she had determined to fight Nicholas every inch of the way; now she just wanted peace, and if that was capitulation of a sort—well, it would have to be blamed on her condition!

But he persisted, saying sardonically, 'I find you difficult to understand. From the missives which I post each week I gather that you've forgiven Rose for her part in our marriage, yet your resentment towards me is unabated.'

'You don't understand. Rose is——' she stopped precipitately.

'Rose is a silly woman,' he finished. 'A silly, mercenary woman who was quite prepared to sell her daughter into slavery so that she and her favourite child could continue to live in the luxury she considers to be their right.'

Alannah winced, for he spoke the truth, yet only part of it. 'You don't understand,' she repeated in a wooden voice.

'I understand very well.' The contempt that hardened his voice made her flush. 'I think it's you who doesn't understand. Rose knew exactly what was going on. I made no attempt to hide my motives or my actions from her.'

'I know.' She sat down, her brows drawn together in a frown as she tried to explain her mother to him. 'Rose has been cossetted and protected all of her life. Dad—Dad used to tease her a little about her lack of interest in financial matters but he made no attempt to change her. She has always believed that if you're positive and look on the bright side then things will work out well.'

She looked up, saw the slight disdainful smile on his mouth and went on passionately, 'It's all very well for you, you don't know what it's like to be valued only for your looks and your charm and your skills as a hostess! Nobody ever encouraged Rose to use her brain. She married Daddy because he was kind and her parents told her he would make her a good husband, and she learned to love him. Naturally she hoped—she was sure that the same thing would happen to me.'

'Even though you were fathoms deep in love with the boy next door?'

The crisp sarcasm made her flinch, but her voice was steady as she retorted, 'She thought it was just a childish crush.'

'And was it?'

The question slashed like an arrow through the air, poison-tipped, aimed to wound. Alannah's mouth went dry. 'You already know the answer to that.'

'Oh, God, yes.' Nicholas laughed deep in his throat and came towards her, stopping so close that the faint salty aroma of him teased her nostrils. 'Love eternal,' he jeered, cupping her chin and forcing her face up to lie open to the savage taunt of his glittering gaze. 'Do you get a secret pleasure from being a martyr, Alannah? Does it console you in the moments when you weep in private that their happiness is due to your sacrifice? Well, I'm not going to deprive you of any legitimate pleasures you get—but remember always that when you lie moaning for release in my arms it's not because you're thinking of Rose's welfare, or Trina's, or your one true love. That reaction belongs to me.'

And he kissed her, forcing her head back against his arm, exploring the depths of her mouth with cruel, sensuous enjoyment until she was trembling with rage and—yes, desire.

When he lifted his head she made a savage gesture of repudiation, wiping her mouth with the back of her hand, her expression glazed with distaste.

He laughed deep in his throat and bit her throat, hard enough to make her jerk. 'I'll do exactly what I want to you,' he said against her skin. 'I leave you alone because I want to, not because I feel I should, and if I want to take you I will, whenever I like.'

'I despise you!'

He smiled, but his eyes were cold and beside his mouth a muscle pulled, once, twice, and then was still. 'I know. I enjoy the way you despise me.'

And watched with the same cruel, knowing gaze as colour heated her skin at this oblique reference to her unabashed response the last time they had loved.

On the Saturday morning Alannah woke with an aching back, an ache which wouldn't go away even after a walk and an hour spent in the pool.

'It's not getting worse, is it?' Ellen asked, frowning. Somewhat surprised by her concern, Alannah wriggled uncomfortably on the sofa.

'No, it's not.'

'Well, I don't know.' Ellen set two cushions straight. 'Oh, don't get worried, it won't be anything, but I think you'd better put your feet up.'

So, restless and cross with herself, Alannah did that, browsing through a pile of books Ellen had brought in from the library. None of them were particularly inspiring. Alannah sighed ostentatiously, drank a cup of tea and tried again to get comfortable. When the telephone rang she reached for it, glad of the interruption.

Not so glad when she heard that distinctive voice at the other end, however. 'Hello, Caroline,' she said.

'Alannah, how are you? Nick tells me you're growing apace.'

Alannah's brows lifted in an ironic salute. 'I am, indeed.'

'Good for you! Could you get Nick for me, please? I'm sorry about disturbing you, but some of the arrangements for the ball tonight have come unstuck and as he's taking me, he'll have to know.'

Alannah bit her lip, but managed to make her voice coolly unconcerned. 'Sorry, but he's not here, Caroline. He's at the flat.'

'Oh.' Came a pause before the smooth, insinuating tones resumed. 'He seems to be spending quite a bit of time down here lately. Pressure of business, I suppose, although he always used to enjoy his weekends at home. Well, I'll hop around and see him. Thanks, Alannah.'

A red tide of anger enveloped Alannah as she put the receiver down. Whatever Caroline's status in Nick's life, and it seemed more and more likely that she was still his mistress, she had no right to be so deliberately provocative. Seething, cursing the fact that she was ungainly and unable to do anything about putting Caroline Sterling in her place, Alannah grimaced and put a hand to the small of her back, arching it.

'That settles it,' Ellen announced from the doorway, 'I'm ringing Dr Stewart.'

And ring him she did, in spite of Alannah's commands to the contrary. He was out within an hour, checked her over and said reassuringly, 'I don't think it's anything at all to be worried about, but stay in bed for a couple of days. Just keep quiet. Now, where's your husband.'

'In Auckland,' Alannah told him curtly.

'He's on his way back,' said Ellen, and at Alannah's astonished query she added crisply, 'He'd have my hide if I didn't tell him!'

On the verge of protesting vigorously, Alannah thought again and closed her mouth.

When Nick arrived she was lying, small and pale in the big bed, watching the sun move across the lawn outside. And only she knew that her pallor was not in any way due to her condition.

'All right?' he asked quickly as he came across the room.

She nodded, feeling guilty and smirched. 'I don't know why there's such a fuss. It's only backache, after all.'

Apparently he had spoken to the doctor, for as he pulled a chair up to the side of the bed he said calmly, 'A backache can be one of the signs of a threatened miscarriage. Stewart doesn't think there's much possibility of that, but he's being cautious.'

'There was no need for you to come back.' Well, if that sounded ungracious, and it did, she couldn't help it. That was the sort of thing he would expect her to say.

He lifted a brow and took one of her hands, kissing it with a gesture which held irony. 'And shock Ellen?'

'Could you?'

He smiled without humour. 'Oh yes, quite easily. She's beginning to hope that proximity might yet accomplish what sex has failed to do, make something of this marriage. We both put on an excellent act for her; but she knows damned well what this baby means to me.'

'Why?'

He shrugged and gave her her hand back. 'The usual reason. Atavism, I suppose, the age-old desire to see my genes reproduced.'

Her curiosity was newborn and therefore strong. 'I read somewhere that all that we are, all of us, body and mind, is just a means of making sure that our genes are handed on. The whole system of things is built around a kind of blind need for the race to survive.'

'And do you believe that?'

She shivered. 'Sometimes. It's a kind of ironic joke, isn't it?'

'One played on you,' said Nicholas, startling her with the sombre intensity of his voice.

It was her turn to look quizzically at him. 'Regretting things, Nick?'

'No,' he said slowly, and stood up to look down at her, dark and dominating. 'No, I don't believe in regrets for the past. They clutter up the present and the future and achieve nothing.' A twisted smile touched the hard line of his mouth. 'Let's just say that I'd do things differently now.'

'Would you still have carried me off?' For some reason she had to know so desperately that it was a real effort to keep her voice light, half amused.

He smiled as though he knew exactly what she was thinking. 'Oh yes, my little piece of plunder. My life would be unbearably dull without you fizzing and erupting in the background. I enjoy having my own small volcano.'

For a moment—horrid, unguarded moment—Alannah thought she was going to shame herself by letting him see the quick, unbidden tears his answer had unaccountably caused. But she managed to hide the suspicious brightness with a quick, faked yawn, turning her head into the pillow.

'I'll leave you,' he said immediately. 'If you want anything, ring.'

She waited until he was almost to the door before saying blandly, 'By the way, did Caroline get you?'

At the sound of her voice he had stopped; now he looked at her over his shoulder, his face expressionless. 'Yes,' he said after a tense moment. 'She was with me when Ellen rang. Why?'

'Oh, just that she rang here for you, so I told her where you were.'

'Did you?' Another odd little pause before he said smoothly, 'Thank you. She must have forgotten that I'd planned to spend the weekend in town.'

Like hell, Alannah thought vulgarly; *she wanted me to know that she was your partner and you know it, you swine!* And she glowered balefully at his broad shoulders until he had gone, leaving her taut, her fingers teasing the soft sheet with quick, fretful movements.

Blast him, what did she care if he slept with Caroline Sterling? When he had first begun to stay away she had welcomed the thought of a mistress. But not one that she knew, she decided angrily, remembering the smug loveliness of the older woman. Nick had no right to bring her here, patronising bitch that she was.

Still, she wasn't going to the ball with him tonight. And although he had said he had come up because of

Ellen she knew a sneaky pleasure at the thought that she could control his actions even if it was with a trick. All traces of guilt had fled when he told her that Caroline had been with him.

No, her backache was definitely not going to get better until tomorrow. Next time perhaps Caroline would think twice before giving rein to her malice!

So she lay cuddled in the bed as the afternoon darkened and clouds swept across the sky. Gurkha, the enormous tabby cat, came tiptoeing across the floor, leapt up on to the bed in defiance of Ellen's strictest rules and rumbled himself—and her—to sleep.

When she awoke it was dark and Nick was standing by the bed smiling down at the pair of them with what almost seemed genuine amusement. Alannah yawned and stretched, then, remembering, put a hand to her back and moved stiffly.

'Still there?'

It hurt to lie, but she managed it. 'A little.' A rattle signified Ellen's arrival with a tray. 'Oh, quick—hide Gurkha——'

But the cat was gone, with one bound removing himself from instant retribution.

Alannah looked up, met quick laughter in Nicholas's eyes and laughed too, a husky, sensuous sound, strangely shy.

'Well, that sounds better,' Ellen commented as she came into the room.

'It's still there,' Nicholas told her lightly. Too lightly.

Alannah looked up in sharp suspicion, but his face was impassive. Relaxing, she pretended to be interested in the contents of the tray. Surely he didn't suspect—no, how could he? If she moved she could still feel a slight ache in the small of her back, so she wasn't really lying. Not really.

CHAPTER EIGHT

AFTER dinner Nicholas brought in a tape deck and several books, more to her taste this time than the ones Ellen had chosen. Then, astoundingly, he pulled up a chair, took out an impressive folder from his briefcase and proceeded to read its contents.

Alannah read for a short time, but her eyes continually found themselves dragged to where her husband sat, dark head slightly bent as he skim-read page after page at an incredible speed, occasionally pausing to jot something down.

Once he looked and caught her watching. For a moment their eyes locked, then she asked for a glass of water, the first thing that came to her mind. He had sat like that on the plane coming up from Christchurch; through the clouds of hatred which had surrounded her she had noticed how fast he read, the spare elegant movements of hand and wrist, the length of his fingers, the hard grace of his body.

If she closed her eyes she could recall every time she had ever seen him, like a movie film in her brain. Deliberately she tried to summon up David's face, but Nick's forceful presence drove him away.

'Anything wrong?'

'No.' Her voice was thick and hesitant. Opening her eyes, she accepted the water and drank it, conscious of his gaze on her downbent head.

'Sure?'

'Quite sure.' She looked up, caught a glimpse of something in his expression and paled. 'I want this baby too,' she said harshly.

'Do you?'

The cool disbelief that hardened his voice made her wince. 'Oh yes,' she retaliated. 'I've carried it around for so long that I'd hate to lose it now. Besides, it's not responsible for its father.'

'No, indeed.'

And that was all. No response to her open incitement. Sighing, Alannah turned her face away from the light and went to sleep.

A long time later she woke. A spatter of rain whirled across the window, driven by an easterly wind. Hugh had predicted a week of it until the wind went right around again, through the north and back to the west. Nickolas had turned off the bedside light and the only one left on was a small lamp which illuminated the bureau which he had bought for the room. Only that day she had written to Rose, the letter lay sealed and stamped on the flap. He stood looking down at it, turning it with his forefinger, his dressing gown loosely belted.

Something in his stance kept her silent and unmoving; she felt as though she was prying into a part of him which should be kept hidden.

Then he lifted his head and she held her breath, for his expression was one of such dark torment that she felt a sudden, unbidden flood of sympathy. Was he thinking of Ngaire, so loved and so longed for?

Years later Alannah was to discover that she grew up in that moment. All that she realised at the time was that the tight bitter core of resentment which had festered within her seemed to evaporate, leaving her empty and forlorn, shaken by her sight of a grief which the years had not eased. Somehow she could see how a man who loved as deeply as Nicholas could cheat and lie and force himself on the cause of his despair, losing all mercy in the progress. Only an immense love could have caused such a savage reaction to his loss.

And with all those other visions of Nicholas, taunting, icily brutal, hard, was that one, Nicholas in an anguish such as she could hardly bear to contemplate.

All desire to hurt him was gone. She closed her eyes again and lay still and quiet while he came across the room and slid beneath the covers. And when his hand reached out to touch hers she did not shrug it away as she would have done earlier. Instead she lay staring into the darkness, unable to rid herself of the picture beneath her eyelids, Nicholas looking as though his very basis of life had been taken from him.

Another milestone in their life together. After this Alannah watched him constantly, trying to fathom out his innermost secrets. Occasionally he caught her, but apart from holding her gaze until she looked away in embarrassment he gave no reaction.

As the year turned slowly towards summer the child within Alannah grew while the distance between its parents remained as great as ever. Bewildered by new emotions which wanted to break through the mask she had fashioned with such effort, Alannah clung to its safety. Nicholas was gentle with her, but there was a depth of reserve in his cool, remote attitude that chilled her. And when she watched him, trying to superimpose that expression of anguish over the cruelly handsome features, so hard with self-command, it was impossible to believe that she had ever seen it. After a while she began to believe it had been a dream.

One day he came home tired, swam for an hour in an expression of strength which awed her before hauling himself up on to the terrace. Alannah tossed him a towel and watched covertly as he dried himself. He was a superb physical specimen, she thought, doing her best to think clinically while a kind of tingling excitement ran across her nerves.

Muscles rippled beneath skin which she now knew to have a natural tan; as he dried his hair he flung his head back and for a moment her mouth dried. He was big, yet he moved so lithely that his size only emphasised the perfect balance of his movements.

If he saw her watching him he gave no indication, but his voice was harsher than it had been for weeks when he spoke.

'I have to go to Australia.'

'Australia?'

'Yes. Melbourne, to be exact.'

Alannah nodded, feeling oddly bereft. He had flown away before, but this time it was too close. Not that she would let him see that, of course.

'When do you go?' she asked politely.

He tossed his coat into a chair. 'The day after tomorrow. I'll be away three or four days, depending.' Perhaps something of her inchoate emotions got through to him, for he said wryly. 'It's only four hours away, Alannah. And Stewart assures me that you're in no danger of having the baby within the next week.'

He came towards her and helped her as she got out of the lounger. 'I have to go,' he said, hands on her shoulders.

Lately she had noticed a disconcerting tendency to rely on him, to lean on his strength. She despised herself for such dependence; it would have to choose this moment to make its reappearance. Tears prickled hot against her eyelids.

'Of course,' she said in that same polite little voice. 'Don't worry, Nick, Ellen watches over me like a dragon.'

His fingers tightened momentarily. 'I know,' he said, half beneath his breath. 'Please believe that I wouldn't go if it weren't absolutely necessary. A lot of people depend on me, and this is important.'

'Of course it is.' She turned away and his hands fell

from her shoulders to his side. For a moment he looked vulnerable, almost torn, and she said coldly, 'For heaven's sake, you're as bad as Ellen! Its only a baby, after all, even if it is the heir to the Challoner fortune. Women have them every day without any fuss at all. Enjoy Melbourne.'

'It's a business trip.' He spoke with the formal precision that meant he was angry.

Alannah hardened her heart. Lately Nicholas had been all that one could ask of the husband of a heavily pregnant woman and it had been perilously sweet to be treated with such consideration, almost as if he quite liked her. It could become addictive. Better by far to remember that she was his possession; any kindness he showed her was a kind of patronage.

When he left he kissed her goodbye because Ellen was there, but the impersonal brush of his lips over hers was totally without warmth. And Alannah wouldn't wave him out of sight.

Hugh Thurkettle drove him down, of course, and brought the car back. It was just sheer bad luck that Alannah should have been afflicted with an unbearable restlessness that evening and tried to assuage it with a walk around the garden when normally she would have been curled up on the lounger basking in the last rays of the sun.

She heard their voices as she ate a white peach, the earliest and sweetest of them all, and made her way towards the vegetable garden. Hugh often worked there until dark; it seemed that tonight Ellen had joined him.

Just when she realised what they were talking about she never afterwards knew. What stopped her behind the feijoa hedge was Ellen's voice, fierce and yet bewildered.

'. . . don't know what he's up to! Taking that wretched Caroline Sterling with him indeed!'

'And her father,' Hugh reminded her.

Ellen's snort was a masterpiece. 'And when has his presence ever had anything to do with anything? He used to come up with her before, and you know what happened then more often than not. If you ask me, old Sterling chooses to show a blind eye because it's good business for him to be in with Nick.'

Hugh grunted something. Above her loudly beating heart Alannah heard Ellen's clearer, more carrying voice and put out a hand to steady herself on the twiggy branches of a feijoa bush.

'I don't know what to think, and that's a fact. Everything seemed to be going along so well. *She's* calmed down, no more tantrums, and he's been good to her—and now *this*! You're sure she was going with him, not just there to see him off?'

No one could have strained her ears so hard as Alannah to hear Hugh's answer, but she could only make out the low rumble of his tones. It was Ellen who confirmed everything.

'Well, that's plain enough,' she said. 'Oh, what on earth is Nick up to?'

Her voice carried on, but Alannah had turned and walked away, moving softly as a sneak-thief through the short, sweet-smelling grass of the orchard, moving by instinct because her eyes were filled with visions of Caroline Sterling in Nicholas's arms. Like a whipped puppy she hurried to hide herself, choosing with sure instinct the one place they would not look for her, the path down the cliff.

Halfway down a knee of pohutukawa formed a rustic seat. Panting, heartsick, Alannah leaned against the rough branch, one hand curled around it, the other pressed to the mound that was Nicholas's child.

For the first time since she had married him tears came, scalding, painful, wrenching at her heart and mind until she slid down to the ground in a heap of anguish and let them flow through her fingers pressed to her face.

The agony was too intense to last long. When it was over she lay quiescent, clenched fists against her throbbing temples, as bewildered by her reactions as Ellen had been by Nicholas's behaviour.

Why? Why should she care whether he took his mistress with him when he travelled? She hadn't cared about anything else he had done, had grown a hard skin against him and been deluded into believing that it had become a part of her.

Now, faced by her sudden collapse, she had to confront her own vulnerable self, the hurt, frightened woman who hid behind temper tantrums and cold restraint because that was the only way she could stay sane in the nightmare Nicholas had created for her.

All that was young and childish rushed to the fore. She wanted Rose, wanted her with a desperation that came close to hysteria, and knew even as she wanted her that there was no one who could give her what she really needed, security and reassurance.

The baby moved; it had been quiet all that day. The flailing within her drove her to her feet. It seemed that she held her breath all the time it took to get her back into her bedroom. The last thing she wanted was Ellen's too-perceptive scrutiny of her pale, swollen face.

Quietly she showered, wishing she could wash away the desolation that ached within her. The bed had never looked more inviting, but it took her a while to get to sleep.

And the pain which woke her was, she knew, a continuation of the pains which had been building in intensity for some time. Nicholas's child had chosen the time of its birth.

An hour later she was tucked up in the labour ward

in the Cottage Hospital with a Sister smiling encouragingly down at her.

'There, you're doing fine,' she said, smoothing back a lock of hair. 'Remembering all of your pre-natal exercises beautifully. This one is definitely in a hurry!'

He was, too. Shortly after dawn had broken Alannah was gazing down at the indignant face of her son, wondering to see features so like Nicholas's stamped on to that tiny countenance, the winged brows, the firm chin, the nose which was going to be as straight and definite as his father's.

The elation which had flooded her ebbed, leaving her tired and cold. Then the baby opened his eyes and some quirk of musculature made it seem as if he smiled at her.

Alannah drew in a sharp, painful breath. Unconsciously her arms tightened and she bent and kissed the soft, wrinkled forehead. Instantly his face turned in blind seeking towards the soft pressure.

'He's hungry,' the Sister said. 'Why don't you feed him?'

Afterwards she slept, waking only when meals were brought to her, until late afternoon. The hospital was small, but she had been put in an annexe off one of the wards and so was alone with her son when Nick strode in.

He was clad in a dark business suit and he looked tired yet formidable, his eyes fixed on Alannah's astonished face.

'How are you?' he asked abruptly.

She swallowed. 'Fine. What—what are you doing here?'

Those brows lifted in cold irony. 'Checking up on my son, what else?'

'You haven't even looked at him.'

He had stopped a pace away from the bed. Now he took that step and tilted her head back, surveying her face with a keen scrutiny until she coloured faintly and her lashes fluttered down.

'Was it bad?' he asked.

The muscles moved in the slender length of her throat. His gentleness almost unmanned her. More than anything she wanted to feel his arms around her, so that she could rest her head on his shoulder and gratefully draw on his strength.

Huskily she said, 'No, it wasn't too bad at all. Dr Stewart said that—that we'll have to be careful with the next one, as this one arrived so quickly. Apparently they usually get faster.'

'If there is a next one.'

He released her and turned away to bend over the crib, leaving her dumbfounded.

Surely that was the whole object of this—this farce of a marriage, to provide him with heirs? Unless he had decided that he wanted no more of her, that Caroline was enough. For some reason Alannah felt such a fury as she hadn't experienced for months . . . Rage, anguish, despair fought for supremacy; leaning back against the pillows, she closed her eyes so that he could not see into them.

'Are you all right?'

'Fine,' she said again, opening her eyes to stare belligerently up at him. 'Well, what do you think of him? Is he enough like you to satisfy the stringent Challoner standards?'

Nicholas shrugged, dark brows drawn together as he watched the sleeping baby. 'Oh, definitely. Tell me, do they always make that peculiar noise?'

Every protective instinct roused, Alannah leaned towards the crib. 'Oh dear,' she said guiltily after a moment. 'Oh, hell!'

She looked just like a schoolgirl caught in some nefarious ploy. A gleam of amusement softened Nicholas's gaze. 'What is it?'

'He's sucking his thumb. And that, I'm afraid, he got from me.'

Nicholas grinned, suddenly much younger looking. 'Well, I guess we'll forgive you. Tell me, what colour are his eyes?' He smiled again at her astonishment. 'Ellen wants to know.'

'But I don't know. At least, they're a sort of milky blue.'

'Baby-coloured eyes,' Sister said briskly as she came into the room with a tray. 'But they'll be blue like yours, Mrs Challoner.'

She bestowed a warm smile on Alannah as she tucked the tray across her knees, another which recognised the fact that Nicholas was a very attractive male on him and left them, no doubt feeling very tactful.

'When are you going back?' Alannah asked, making no attempt to lift the covers from the plates. 'I presume Mr Sterling is filling in for you?'

Nicholas's gaze sharpened, lancing across the room. 'No, he's not. I have to go back on tonight's flight. Who told you that Ralph was with me?'

'Oh, I overheard Ellen and Hugh talking,' she said airily. 'Caroline's enjoying herself, is she?'

That hard stare intensified. 'Very much,' he said with spiky emphasis.

There was a pause, tense but brief because Alannah filled it by removing the cover from a bowl of soup.

Nicholas moved so silently that she started when his hand over hers prevented her from picking up the spoon.

'Nothing to say?' he asked.

'N-no.' It was cowardly; it was also the only sensible response. She recognised that controlled menace.

'Well, I'll leave you.' His hand moved, slid up to cup her breast. 'Goodbye, my darling wife,' he whispered, bending his head to force a kiss on her unresponsive lips.

It was openly lustful, as was the touch of his thumb across her nipple, emphasising the sensual prison she lived in. Alannah hated him, especially as in some basic level it won a response, startling in its intensity.

When he stood his skin was flushed across his cheekbones and she shrank back against the pillows, for it seemed to her that hatred glinted beneath the heavy lids.

Quickly, before she had time to think, she asked, 'Are you going straight back?'

'Yes.'

'Won't you be tired?'

He shrugged, a sneer twisting his lips. 'Since when has my welfare worried you?'

And he was gone, leaving her to bite on her lip, astonished and exhausted.

The hospital stretched their rules over the next few days, letting Ellen visit her.

'Usually,' said the Sister, 'we make it family only, but we're a reasonable lot.'

'When,' asked Ellen after Alannah had exclaimed over an exquisitely smocked romper suit, 'when is your mother coming up?'

Alannah chuckled. 'I haven't the faintest idea, but she's waiting until Trina's year finishes. She's sent me the most involved telegram I've ever read, but I think it means they'll be here tomorrow or the day after. She also sent me two lots of flowers and a long letter which is also very inscrutable. Rose is not good at moments of high drama, which is evidently what she has decided this is to be.'

'Well, you must admit there were dramatic elements.'

When she had left Alannah sighed, looking around at the flower-filled ward with unseeing eyes. She felt tired, weary to the bones and lonely. Since the baby's birth she had been weepy and depressed. And she wanted her mother. Or the childhood security that Rose represented.

The next day Nicholas arrived back, waiting for an hour at the airport to pick up Rose and Trina. The first Alannah knew of either event was laughter outside her door, followed by a coy tapping.

It was her mother, and with her Trina, somehow older and infinitely more mature. Alannah stared at them, then horrified herself by bursting into tears.

'Darling!' Rose exclaimed, hurrying across to pat her daughter's hand.

But it was Trina who sat on the bed and put her arm around the slender shoulders and pressed a soft cheek to Alannah's until the sobs ceased shaking her body.

'Oh, I'm being so stupid! Whatever must you think!'

'Post-natal blues,' Rose said comfortably. 'It happens to everyone. I remember crying buckets when I brought you home from hospital. Your poor father thought he had a madwoman on his hands!'

Talking, chatting easily, she kept tension at bay until Alannah had wiped her eyes and blown her nose and recovered some of her composure. Trina rose quietly and took the other chair, her regard grave as she watched her mother and sister.

'I'm fine,' Alannah protested, leaning back on the pillows. 'Very spoiled. Have you seen my son?'

'We've only just got here!' Rose smiled. 'What are you going to call him?'

'I don't know yet.' Suddenly it seemed tragic not to have any idea of what her child's name was to be, and she felt her fingers pleating the sheet as she hurried on. 'After Daddy, but Nicholas hasn't decided what his first name is to be.'

The sound of a trolley made a welcome interruption,

especially as the trolley proved to be Master Challoner's crib, pushed by a smiling nurse.

'Here you are,' she said. 'Hungry as the proverbial hunter!'

While he suckled Rose averted her eyes, strangely embarrassed by such a natural process, but Trina smiled for the first time.

'He's tiny,' she said softly.

Alannah frowned with mock-indignation. 'I'll have you know he's bigger than your average child,' she told her loftily, adding with a perfect imitation of one particular doting mother who had infuriated them often, 'And so *advanced* for his age!'

And she laughed at the look on her sister's face, the rich, infectious sound dragging her son from his greedy absorption so that he opened his eyes, still baby-grey but the same shape and setting as his father's. And on cue, Nicholas walked in.

'Why, he's going to have blue eyes,' Rose exclaimed. 'Just like yours, darling. How lovely!'

It was the first time Nicholas had seen his son nursing. Sudden colour flicked Alannah's skin as his eyes rested for a moment on the tender swell of her breast; it took her all her will-power not to twitch up a fold of her bedjacket. He recognised her dilemma and smiled with hard irony. Then he bent and brushed her mouth with his. His lips were warm and with one finger he touched the round curve of his son's cheek. The baby stared up at him, one tiny hand pressed to the silken warmth of Alannah's breast before closing his eyes and resuming business.

'He's a darling,' Rose said warmly, while Trina's gaze moved from Nicholas to Alannah and back again. 'And so like you, Nick! But tell me, what are you going to call him? Alannah, silly girl, doesn't seem to have any idea!'

'Andrew Holman. After both grandfathers.'

Rose's eyes filled with easy tears. 'Thank you,' she said emotionally. 'My dear Holt would have been so proud to see his first grandchild. But just don't dare call your little daughter Rose! I've always hated my name and I couldn't bear the thought of someone else being lumbered with it!'

Heat rose to Alannah's throat. She didn't dare look beyond her son's beatific expression as Nicholas made a teasing rejoinder, but she was conscious of Trina's gaze on her downcast face.

She was also conscious of the fact that her hair hadn't yet recovered its gloss, that all the evidence of the tiring process of giving birth had not yet been erased from her face and skin. And here was Rose talking of another child!

'. . . quite close together so that they can be friends and companions, just as you and Trina were,' she finished complacently.

It was Nicholas who spoke. 'Alannah had a rugged time during this pregnancy,' he said, somehow making it a definite statement of intent, 'so we'll wait a while before we subject her to that again.'

'Oh, but the second time is usually much easier to cope with,' Rose declared knowledgeably, then fell silent at something in Nicholas's glance.

Trina dropped a comment into the odd little hush, effectively filling it until it was time to burp Andrew and Rose demanded the privilege and some of the tension eased from the atmosphere. But then, and later that night when she lay for the last time in the hospital bed, Alannah wondered if Nicholas's statement meant that he would not expect to make love to her again until he thought it desirable to have another child. And slow, hot tears coursed down her cheeks as she listened to the subdued noise of the traffic outside and the odd, unconnected sounds in the hospital.

The staff made a little production of sending their

patients off, Sister ceremoniously handing Andrew over to his mother while other nurses wished them goodbye and sent swift, admiring sideways glances at Nicholas from beneath their lashes.

He did all that a new father should have done, thanked them with his aloof charm, handed something over in an envelope for the new T.V. in the nurses' home and at just the right moment swept his wife and son into the car.

All the way home Alannah looked down at the baby's sleeping face, noted the strong framework beneath the soft, fine skin, the incipient arrogance which was a legacy from his father.

'Tired?'

She shook her head. 'No.'

'Just let down.' At her surprised glance he smiled austerely. 'Stewart warned me that you'd probably slip into depression and would need careful handling for the next few weeks.'

'And are you going to—handle me carefully?'

He was silent for long enough to make her wonder why she persisted in gibing at him, but when he answered his voice was weary. 'I don't intend to handle you at all, if you've been worrying about that. You've made your feelings on the subject more than clear.'

Strapped into the carrycot in the back seat, Andrew made an indeterminate noise. Alannah twisted anxiously around to make sure that he was all right. When she turned back Nicholas's hands were clenched tightly on to the wheel so that the knuckles showed white.

'You must think I'm some kind of monster,' he said acidly. 'You've just had nine months of misery; do you really expect me to put you through the same thing again without giving you a breathing space?'

Alannah watched as his grip relaxed. 'You haven't exactly set out to—to endear yourself,' she said hesitantly.

'No.' A grim smile tightened his mouth. 'That was the last thing I intended. I wanted to cow you thoroughly, break you. Only you refused to break, didn't you? Every time I tried, you sprang back, eyes shooting sparks, your tongue dripping venom. Why aren't you frightened of me, Alannah?'

She gazed unseeingly out of the window. 'I don't know. I was, sometimes. Only I knew that whatever you did, if I didn't allow it to happen you couldn't hurt me.' She shrugged. 'You made an error in judgment there. If you'd really wanted to hurt me you should have persuaded me into falling in love with you and then done your Demon King act.'

'That,' he told her calmly as he turned the car into their road, 'was my original idea.'

Alannah's head whipped around. The hard, handsome profile was impassive, but irony tugged at the corner of his mouth.

'Then I discovered that you had a boy-friend,' he finished. 'So I had to use force.'

He turned, flicked her a swift glance before concentrating once more on the narrow, winding hill. Alannah looked down at her hands, tightly clasped in her lap. Uneasiness gnawed at her. Why was he so—so open with her?

But he said no more, and by then they were almost home and the moment was past. And then there was the subdued but excited welcome from those who awaited them, and Alannah's discovery that the crib had been set up in the nursery, two doors away.

Clutching her baby to her breast, she shook her head, looking her most stubborn.

'No,' she said clearly. 'If he sleeps in here so shall I.' She delivered the ultimatum in a voice that trembled, but the challenge in her eyes as she gazed at them all was very steady.

'Very well,' said Nick, and smiled at the astonishment she couldn't hide. 'At night he'll sleep in our room until you're over your nervousness.'

It had been as simple as that. Indeed, as she sank thankfully into bed that evening she found herself still astounded at the ease of her victory. Nicholas must be taking Dr Stewart's injunction to heart, because this was definitely kid glove treatment!

Ellen had insisted that she go to bed early, and indeed, she felt herself sinking beneath waves of exhaustion. Now with only the soft light of the bedside lamp pooling around her she lay for a moment, her eyes on the outline of the crib. Rose had brought up the elaborate ribboned drapes which had decorated both Alannah's and Trina's cribs and lovingly remade them for Andrew, threading blue ribbon through the lace, hemming a drift of mosquito netting with more ribbon and lace.

Alannah turned the lamp off, settling back into the pillows with a sigh. Life suddenly seemed unbearably bleak, and it didn't help to tell herself that this would pass. Some of her weepiness might stem from those post-natal blues Rose had evoked so glibly, but more from the cold scar which had formed over her emotions.

Shivering, she thought fancifully that she would never feel warm again. Pampered, her every material need indulged, she knew a devouring emptiness which not even her fierce protective love for the child could fill.

That night she dreamt that she and David were walking along the high, rolling curves of the Cashmere Hills. It was a clear day and the Southern Alps gleamed like a fairytale across the Canterbury Plains. David's hand held hers in its warm grip and they walked without talking along a path just wide enough for the two of them. Then the path forked, one way continuing into the hills, the other leading towards what she knew, in the way of dreams, to be a place of great danger.

'I have to leave you now,' she said to David, and walked away from him, making her way down towards the danger which loomed ahead. Twice he called after her, but she knew that his path was the easy pleasant path where skylarks sang and the wind blew free, so she didn't answer.

But she woke, crying, his name on her lips. And Nicholas was standing beside the bed, hands stuffed into the pockets of his jacket as though he had to keep them there or strike her. He looked as if he was carved from granite.

Alannah gasped, covering her face with her hands while the tears seeped down through her fingers, and after a moment he sat down on the bed and lifted her up to hold her gently against him.

'It's all right,' he said soothingly when she stiffened with fright.

But she knew that she had reason for her fear. In that split second before she had hidden her face there had been murder in his gaze.

'Sh,' he whispered, smoothing her shoulders and back. 'It's all right, Alannah. Everything will be fine,' and when she choked he teased, 'You'll wake the baby!'

She made a funny noise in her throat, but that worked and she quietened down, oddly comforted by the soothing stroking movements of his hands over her skin.

'O.K. now?'

'Yes,' she breathed.

He set her back against the pillows and walked away. Faint noises from the dressing room revealed his progress towards bed. He had taken two steps back into the bedroom when Andrew gave a small sighing cry. Nicholas froze; so did Alannah. Snuffles and a snort or two followed, but nothing more. After a few moments Nicholas resumed his passage towards the bed. Alannah tried to breathe deeply and evenly while her heart thumped with unmerciful force.

As he slid in between the sheets he said mockingly, 'Goodnight, Alannah,' then disposed himself for sleep, and seemed to reach that enviable state in no time flat while Alannah lay stiff with tension.

At last a sad smile touched her lips; she moved her hand tentatively across the no-man's-land between them until it touched his and at last joined him in sleep.

When she woke it was still early—very early, and Andrew was winding up for another bellow.

'What——? Oh, hell!' Nicholas's voice had all the startled chagrin of any new father woken for the first time by a hungry baby. Alannah was busy trying to break free from his grip, one arm beneath her neck, the other across her waist, his hand cupping her breast. How had they got like this, with his body curved around hers so—so lovingly?

No time to think of it, anyway, for their son was hungry and determined to let the world know about it. As soon as Nicholas's grip slackened Alannah was out of the bed and across the room without thinking of a dressing-gown.

'Hey there,' she murmured into the truculent little face. 'Calm down, sweetie.'

And now there was another pitfall to be negotiated. With the baby nuzzling fiercely at her breast she looked across to where her husband lay.

'Come back to bed,' he commanded softly.

'I can sit in the chair.'

He smiled. 'The chair is in the nursery. You wanted him in here, you nurse him in here. And get back into bed before you catch a chill.'

Anger lit sparks in her eyes. Oh, she should have known that yesterday's victory had come too easily.

'Very well, then,' she snapped, spitting the words out. 'Here!'

And she deposited a cross Andrew into the bed beside his father, then turned and ran into the bathroom to get a glass of water.

When she came back they looked very comfortable, the tiny dark head of the baby resting against his father's shoulder as Nicholas spoke softly to him.

She pushed the pillows up and got in, angry and embarrassed, yet aware of a deep inner pleasure at the sight of them together.

'I'm ready,' she said, taking the baby as he was held up to her.

It took only a few minutes for the turmoil of her emotions to drain away. Beside her Nicholas lay, eyes fixed intently on her as outside the world lightened into day.

'Can't you get back to sleep?' she asked at last.

He shrugged. 'It doesn't seem worth it. I've no doubt you'd wake me when you put him back.'

She sighed. 'It's not going to work out, is it, this having him sleep in here. I suppose I'm just being stupid and—and over-protective.'

'Certainly,' he agreed with maddening promptness. 'But if you're going to lie awake all night worrying about him then he'll have to stay.'

Slanting a swift downwards glance at him Alannah could make nothing of his expression. He was more than usually impassive.

'But I don't want you to be disturbed,' she said, tension hardening her voice.

He smiled. 'How considerate of you! Or is it that you'd rather not let me see you like that? You can't hide from me all the time, Alannah, so it will pay to get used to my presence when you feed him.'

'No,' she protested, conscious of the flick of anger in his voice. 'It wasn't that—I didn't even think of——'

'Oh, forget it.' He turned his head, effectively shutting her out. 'I'll try not to let my smirching gaze linger too long on your—er—feminine attributes, my dear, but I'm damned if I'm going to avert my gaze like a selfconscious teenager every time I happen to be around when my son is hungry!'

The blighting sarcasm in his tones made her wince; tears gathered beneath her lashes as she hugged the baby closer to her.

Whatever she did was wrong, it seemed. And because she didn't want him to know that his anger made her voice tremble she stayed silent while birds sang the dawn in with riotous pleasure.

CHAPTER NINE

ANDREW was a good baby. Rose said so and even Ellen said so, and she should know. He slept when he was supposed to and woke at roughly four-hour intervals during the day, and grew and gazed at the world about him with great, mildly surprised eyes.

And all about him summer dreamed across the estuary, bringing another kind of growth. Crowds of holidaymakers camped in the bays and lived in small cottages or moved into the few palatial establishments which could be dignified as seaside homes but were always referred to as baches. Every farmhouse sprouted tents like peculiar mushrooms and up and down the river slipped graceful yachts and cheeky runabouts and dignified launches. Water-skiers as small and rigid as dolls flashed back and forth across the glittering, dancing waters, children swam and paddled and dug holes in the sand, windsurfers flew and collapsed like broken butterflies.

It was another world. Although Puhinui was not invaded by the hordes their presence was inescapable, especially as Trina was adopted by a group who anchored in the bay at Nick's invitation and there were barbecues on the beach and pipi-picking parties and days when she was out from soon after breakfast to late at night.

The yachties were a cheerful, happy-go-lucky group, friends of Nick's who accepted Alannah and the baby with astounding lack of comment.

Rose was happy. Once she had assured herself of the impeccable social standing of the yacht owners, a process which involved an extensive exploration of family trees and the discovery that a second cousin somewhere had married someone's goddaughter, she was able to devote herself to her grandson. And to helping Ellen. Surprisingly, for Alannah if not for anyone else, Ellen permitted her help. Occasionally Alannah saw a dry amusement in the housekeeper's regard when she watched Rose, but relations were amicable.

Alannah found herself drifting. The despair which had struck her on her arrival home had faded to a quiet melancholy. As the long, hot weeks went by, she accepted it as part of her life. With her figure regained and her strength returned she refused to be cosseted by Rose any longer.

Nicholas had retreated to some unreachable place. The mockery was back but muted, as if he no longer cared enough about her to want to hurt her. He began introducing her to the people of the area, using a regatta three bays along to take the initial step. Invitations arrived; he accepted them, assuring Alannah that Andrew would be as welcome at a party as his parents.

He was correct. Slowly she began to recognise the people she saw in the street.

One day he told her casually that he had opened an account for her at the bank. But he still refused to allow her to drive, and after a few close shaves she accepted his edict, though rebelliously. She was a good driver, but common sense told her that many of the cars she met were likely to be driven by others who had as little experience as she on the narrow, winding roads.

Apparently his reasons for keeping her a prisoner in his house no longer existed. Alannah wondered and watched him, her expression controlled as she absorbed everything about him, the way he laughed and teased Trina, the respect he evoked from his neighbours, even the glint of appreciation in feminine eyes when they rested on his tall elegance. And she did not know why she watched him.

Then one day he took the big car and set off for Auckland, returning several hours later with someone in the front seat beside him.

'Did you know?' Alannah hissed at Ellen as she dragged a sun-frock over her bikini.

'Yes, I knew,' Ellen returned without expression.

'How long is he staying?'

'Nick didn't say.'

Alannah pushed her fingers through her curls, riotous and still damp after a session in the pool. 'Blast the man, he might——' Her voice cracked as her incredulous eyes took in the tall slim figure beside Nick.

'*David!*' she gasped, and only Ellen's sudden grab at her arm stopped her from running towards him and flinging herself into his arms.

Fortunately they were far enough away for her to regain some small amount of composure—and, with any luck, for her involuntary betrayal to have been overlooked—but the single glance she gave her husband was icy with reproach and resentment.

He looked the same, good-looking, kind and, beside Nick, very young. As they came towards her across the wide flagged atrium beneath the white sweet-scented mandevilla vine Alannah lifted her chin and held out her hand, saying calmly, 'Dear David, how lovely to see you!'

He took her hand, but only after a momentary hesitation that made her sick with anger. David didn't want to upset Nicholas.

'You look—wonderful,' he said with quiet emphasis. 'You—your husband tells me you're a mother now.'

She refused to look at Nicholas, not trusting herself, although she could sense his presence, darkly dominating.

'Don't sound so surprised,' she said, falsely bright. 'Andrew is over a month old now.'

'Congratulations.' He looked around him, hiding his unease. 'This is a beautiful home you have here.'

'Thank you.' At last she looked at Nicholas to meet a glance of such bored indifference that it was as though he had slapped her in the face. 'You must be hot and tired. Did you fly in today? Would you like something to drink before we show you where your room is?'

'I'd rather have a shower,' said David with a frankness which somehow struck her as youthful. 'Fourteen hours in a jet is inclined to leave you feeling sticky and crumpled.'

'I can imagine.'

Nicholas said coolly, 'I'll show you your room. Come out on to the terrace when you've freshened up and we'll give you a drink.'

When they had gone Alannah sank down on to a chair, her face paper-white as she fought for control. Her main emotion was a searing, white-hot anger which made her eyes blaze and her hands shake with the desire to feel Nick's throat between them.

How dared he! As if he hadn't done enough! To wait until she had achieved a precarious kind of stability and then wilfully, *deliberately*, confront her with David. Oh, how *dared* he!

'Very easily,' Ellen said drily. 'You should know the man you married well enough by now to be aware that there's nothing he wouldn't dare—if the odds were right.'

It was no use trying to hide anything from Ellen. 'But *why*?' Alannah whispered numbly, shock replacing anger as she stared up at the older woman. 'He must be mad!'

'I wouldn't bank on it. Nick's got a brain like a trap, cold, clever and remorseless. He'll tell you what he's up to in his own good time.'

'My God, I could kill him!'

'Not for the first time, and you got over the other times.' Ellen smiled with immense irony. 'Oh yes, you did, so don't shake your head at me like that. For what it's worth, I think Nick's forcing the pace. Basically he's as impatient as the next man, for all that he's usually prepared to wait for what he wants. I think this time he's sick of waiting.'

'But what does he want?' Alannah closed her eyes briefly. 'He's got everything he wants.'

'Has he?' On occasions Ellen liked being cryptic. It was infuriating that this should be one of those occasions. 'Hadn't you better do something to that hair?' she added. 'It looks as if your curls want to take off into orbit!'

Alannah muttered something uncomplimentary about her hair and the world in general, but took the hint, walking wearily back to the bedroom. Trina and Rose had spent the day out on the yacht but would be back soon, and they would sit beneath the wide pergola which sheltered the atrium and amidst the perfumed ambience of summer jasmine and mandevilla they would drink something cool and talk over their day.

And Nicholas would be as he always was, suave, so worldly and sophisticated that the turbulence which he had created would die away into a kind of calm. But *why*? Oh, he was a cruel, cruel devil, and she hated him!

For David she dressed carefully in an outfit her mother had objected to, calling it too juvenile. But for once, Alannah thought, surveying herself in the mirror, Rose had been wrong. The loose blue and white striped linen blouse revealed a little more décolletage than would be acceptable for a schoolgirl even with the far from sensual nursing bra she wore. Over it was a casual little pinstriped waistcoat and the cotton skirt was splashed with a muted flower print in blue and grey and white, the full skirt edged with a border of the same material as the waistcoat. The fresh, pretty blue emphasised her eyes and the vivid dancing texture of her hair; as she sprayed herself with *Magie Noire* she frowned. The fragrance was her favourite, a sophisticated blend of Bulgarian rose and spicy, woody perfume, and it seemed an age since she had worn it. For a moment she stood at the dressing table, her small face set in worry and pain, then she straightened her shoulders.

Whatever Nicholas intended by this latest refinement of torture she would not give him the pleasure of seeing how affected she was. And in spite of everything, at the thought of seeing David again her heart lifted, expanded within her breast. Although her mouth was firm with control, deep in her eyes there was a sparkle which she had thought long dead.

That evening Nicholas was at his most urbane. Puzzled and suspicious, Alannah's gaze constantly followed him. An inch or so shorter than David, his lithe elegance somehow made the younger man seem too tall, almost gawky and awkward. Not that David was at too much of a disadvantage. After a tense few minutes when confronted by Rose and Trina he allowed himself to be wooed into relaxation by the sophisticated ambience about him.

Alannah found it impossible to relax. Taut, every nerve stretched, she drank Perrier water and lemon, listening to the soft tinkle of ice in each glass, while Nicholas led David on to talk of his job. She was not in the least surprised at the respect which gradually infiltrated David's voice. Naturally Nicholas would be able to discuss computers with him, just as he was able to swap farm talk with his neighbours and making biting, intelligent criticisms of literature and music. That cold, clear brain wasn't clouded by the emotions that tended to clutter up lesser people's thinking.

On the surface it was a pleasantly civilised evening. Dinner was superb, they talked and laughed, Trina coaxed David into the pool for a swim, and after that they sat in the dark and talked some more while far enough away a partying group of holidaymakers played light pop to make a pleasant background.

Their voices were muted. Nicholas sat beside Alannah on the sofa, but made no attempt to touch her.

When they were alone in their bedroom she turned on him, eyes flashing. But before she could speak he held up a hand.

'You'll wake the baby.'

Her lips tightened, but she couldn't prevent a swift glance at the crib and when she spoke her voice was low, throbbing with an emotion she barely understood. 'You know bloody well he sleeps like a log. What the *hell* do you mean by bringing David here?'

'I don't like to hear you swear.' His hand shot out, caught her chin and twisted it up. 'Don't do it again. As for the boy-friend—well, you've been a docile little creature lately. I thought I'd reward you.'

Frightened by the cold malice in his tones, she stared upwards, but the light was behind him and she couldn't make out any expression on his face at all.

'I think I could kill you,' she whispered at last in a trembling voice.

There was a flash of white as he smiled. 'I enjoy that thread of violence just beneath the surface. It's so at variance with your sweet schoolgirlish face and body. Hate away, Alannah. At least it's a more vigorous emotion than the wishy-washy affection you feel for that boy out there.'

'I love David.'

'Do you?' he said indifferently, refusing to release

his hold of her chin. 'Do you know, darling, I doubt that.'

'You'd like me to fall in love with you, wouldn't you?' she flashed back furiously. 'Then you'd really be revenged for Ngaire's death!'

'I don't blame you for her death,' he said without expression as he turned, his hand dropping away from her face.

Alannah sat down abruptly on the bed. 'I—*what* did you say?'

He began the nightly transference of the contents of his pockets to the bedside table. 'I never did,' he told her. 'Oh, for a few weeks, until the inquest, but it was clear enough what had happened. There were faults on both sides.'

Pressing her hands to her temples to quell the tumult there, Alannah asked faintly, 'But—but you *said*—you said that that was why I had to marry you. You *said* it was my fault.'

'I know.' He glanced across the bed, his expression shuttered. 'And the reason for that is the reason why David Opie is here.'

Nothing made sense. 'I don't understand,' Alannah said wearily.

'I know you don't. Perhaps if you stopped dwelling on your wrongs and looked outwards for a few minutes each day you might.'

This, delivered in his most bored tones, fired her up again. 'Haven't I reason——?'

'Will you *shut* up?' He sounded more than bored now. That shrivelling contempt was plain in the deep voice as he walked across to the door. 'Just go to bed,' he advised as he reached it. 'I've work to do.'

Heaven knew what time he finally made it to bed. Alannah lay awake for hours, but there was no sign of him, and when Andrew woke them at his usual ungodly hour Nicholas didn't stir, lying twisted away from her so that only the dark contour of his head and the wide, brown shoulders were visible above the long lean line of his back.

Dawn brought no counsel to Alannah. Restless, tired yet unable to go back to sleep, she slipped into a bikini and a towelling jacket. A swim might freshen her up.

Some desire for the cleansing of the sea impelled her down the path to the bay. The water was cool but invigorating, the estuary more beautiful than she had ever seen it in its tranquillity. On the hills sheep baaed softly as they formed single files and followed each other along narrow tracks. Shags, black and delinquent, dried their wings on the piles of the jetty and a blue heron flew in slow, serene flaps across to the other side.

Alannah walked up on to the sand, wringing her clustering curls free of sea-water, her small figure gilded by the sun and the water.

'Hello,' said David uncertainly from the cliff path.

'Oh!' She felt herself colouring. Ridiculous to be so embarrassed. David had seen her in a bikini hundreds of times. Nevertheless, moving with considerably less than her usual grace she jammed herself into her jacket, hauling the belt tight around her narrow waist before she looked at him.

He was leaning against the pohutukawa tree, hands tucked into his trouser pockets, smiling at her with a quizzical lift of his brows. 'Sorry, I didn't mean to give you a fright.'

'Just made me jump. I wasn't expecting anyone.'

'Mr—your husband doesn't get up early?'

Something prickled across her skin. 'Normally he would, but he worked late last night.'

David shifted feet, looking down between them. Like her, he seemed uneasy and bewildered. It hardly seemed possible that after their long years of loving companionship they should be reduced to banalities like this instead of conversation.

'He's got a brilliant mind,' he said suddenly.

Alannah nodded. This was high praise indeed.

'When I got your letter I—well, I was hurt and very upset. I thought—I'd hoped that after the two years we could get married.' He looked up, catching her expression. 'It wasn't so long to wait,' he said defensively, 'And you were so young.'

'Yes, of course.' Could this be her, speaking so quietly while within her her heart was breaking?

'Lately I've been able to see things from your point of view. And meeting him—well, I can understand how he swept you off your feet. He's got everything going for him, hasn't he?'

Yes, that was a hint of hero-worship in expression.

Tonelessly Alannah said, 'Oh, he has indeed.'

The sun gleamed on the thick thatch of blond hair as he nodded. 'So it's all for the best, really, isn't it? You have to admire him, getting rid of me like that! He told me on the way up yesterday that he's going to make the scholarship permanent. He owns a firm that has just developed some interesting new components.'

Sick at heart, Alannah began to walk past him. So Nick had held out the possibility of an exciting position for David and David had taken the subtle hint. Fragments of memories hit her like small blows.

'You are the lover,' Nick had taunted, 'he the loved one.'

He had been right. She had never recognised the quick opportunism that lay like a flaw in David's character amidst the kindness and the good humour. Nick had though, and used it to achieve his own ends, just as David was here for a purpose now. Devil, devil, her heart cried as she exchanged meaningless remarks with this man she had thought she loved—no, she corrected fiercely, she had loved him with a child's wholehearted idealism.

At the top of the cliff David said cheerfully, 'I'm glad you're happy, Alannah. Not that many people would be miserable in such magnificent surroundings,' with an appreciative, rather covetous glance around him.

Well, she knew of one.

'You've matured,' he went on. 'You're quieter. Motherhood, I suppose. It seems to have worked wonders in taming that temper, too.'

If he had been able to see into her head he would have realised just how far from the mark he was. But she smiled and left him and walked across the dew-wet grass to the terrace outside the bedroom. The clematis she had chosen to plant for shade were still only tiny vines. Next year they would be halfway up the supports, and the year after that . . .

It made no sense. Nothing made sense any longer. For as long as she could remember she had loved David, first as a brother then as a man, and now she no longer did. He smiled at her and nothing happened, no glow, no deep warmth at his presence. It was gone like the dead leaves of autumn and she felt a grief as deep as that which had struck her at her father's death.

Once in the bedroom she walked across to the crib. Andrew was awake, as he often was at this time, staring with near-sighed interest at one small starfish hand. She smiled and looked across at the empty bed, hating it, hating this room and this beautiful house, hating her husband most of all, because she knew now why he had brought David back.

'Did you have a pleasant tête-à-tête?'

At the sound of his taunting voice she swung around, and all her grief and bewilderment came to a climax. He had just shaved and wore that peculiarly satisfied look of a man whose dearest plans have just come to fruition.

She could have killed him, but it was stupid to give way to her emotion. 'Pleasant enough,' she said stonily. 'Why did you bring him back, Nick?'

His eyes were narrowed as they probed her face. 'Oh, I think you know,' he replied with calm effrontery.

'You're very clever.' Bitterness hardened her tones. 'Well, it worked. Now you've stripped me of my only little memory of romance. I hope you're happy. You deserve to be—you've worked hard enough for this result. I don't think I have ever despised anyone as much as I despise you!'

The glitter of colour beneath his lashes deepened, but he said nothing, and after a moment turned and left her alone in the big room with her son waving his innocent hands before his eyes.

Alannah bit her lip to stop the tears and with head held high went into the bathroom to shower and wash her hair. She and Andrew had an appointment with the doctor that morning.

On the surface breakfast was a perfectly pleasant meal, but Alannah felt Trina's eyes on her too often to be normal and David seemed to be hiding a lack of ease. Rose spread her usual cloak of lighthearted charm over an uncomfortable meal and Nick was his usual confident self. But it was Hugh who drove Alannah and Andrew in to the doctor's and when they arrived back, tired after an unusually long wait, Nicholas was nowhere to be seen.

In fact, there was no one in the house but Ellen, and she was unhelpful.

'I think they're out on the yacht,' she said when Alannah asked her. 'How did the trip to the doctor's go?'

'Oh, fine. Andrew is one hundred per cent, and so am I.' Alannah managed a smile.

'You don't look it. Why don't you have a rest? I'll bring your lunch in ten minutes or so.'

'No, I can't do that. You've enough to do.'

But Ellen was adamant, so Alannah ate it and discovered that she was tired enough to sleep until the baby demanded food.

It was hot, hotter than any day so far. The sun beat the waters of the estuary into a smooth metallic sheet, silencing by its force all the myriad sounds. Even the breeze which made morning and evening so pleasant had stilled.

Alannah lay back on the bed, her son resting sweetly in her arms. She wore a bikini and he had on only a thin cotton petticoat; even so the small dark head was damp, but he was such a beloved weight that she had yielded to temptation and kept him by her. Her eyes roamed his small form with an intensity of emotion that brought a film of moisture to her glance. He was so tiny yet so lusty, growing apace. One day he would be as big as his father, tall and strong and powerful, only, please God, not with that granite centre.

Yawning, she pressed her cheek against his, smiling as he made a funny little grimace. Across the room the mirror reflected them, a very modern mother and child.

A shadow outside jerked her head around. When Nicholas came through the door her lips tightened into an ominous line.

'Relax,' he said quietly. 'I've just put David on the plane for Christchurch. He sends all that's polite.'

Whatever she had expected it was not that!

'Trina has gone with him,' he continued, coming across to stand by the bed. 'She'll stay with his parents until your mother goes back.'

Alannah looked up into the impassive mask of his face, searching vainly for something, some expression. There was a long pause before he resumed, 'If you want to you can go back with Rose.'

For a moment she couldn't credit what her ears had

heard. Her heart thumped heavily in her breast, then began to beat with slow painful thuds.

'For—for how long?' she asked hoarsely.

'As long as you like. For ever, if that's the way you want it.'

It was like a death knell. 'You know I can't leave Andrew,' she whispered, hugging the baby closely to her breast.

Still in the same even toneless voice he said, 'You may take him with you.'

For a period of time it seemed that the world stopped. Alannah's eyes stretched so widely open that they hurt, but she could read nothing in his face. Words would not come past the roughness in her throat.

'All that I ask,' Nicholas went on flatly, 'is that you allow me access to him—and that several times a year you bring him here so that I—so that he grows up knowing me.'

'Why?'

The broad shoulders lifted in a shrug. Very coldly he said, 'He's likely to be the only child I'll have. I don't want him to be a stranger to me.'

'Why?' she whispered. 'Why are you letting me go?'

He shoved his hands into his pockets, hunching his shoulders slightly. 'Because I didn't intend you to be so unhappy,' he said composedly. 'You've called me conceited several times—possibly I am. Perhaps money corrupts in less obvious ways than those usually quoted. I've never had any difficulty in getting any woman I wanted. I assumed that after the first indignant outcry you'd be the same. I didn't bargain for a will as strong as my own. So you have won. You may go.'

Then he added mockingly, 'But I wouldn't take up with Opie again. He's a nice chap, but he's too easy-going for you. And he's going to love Trina when she decides to let him.'

Alannah sat up, indignation flushing her cheeks. 'Oh, you are a mocking devil!' she spat.

Something flamed behind the green eyes. With a twisted smile he said 'No, he definitely couldn't cope with you! Here——' putting his hand in his pocket he drew out a glittering strand and tossed it so that it landed on her lap, 'take this as a souvenir. I hope it recompenses you for a miserable year.'

Alannah looked with baffled anger at him, then at the necklace, then at the sleeping face of her son. The necklace was heavy and cold across her bare thighs, a large green stone with diamonds around it depending from a gold chain set with more diamonds. The stone was carved into the likeness of a barbaric mask. Rich yet primitive, strangely sophisticated, it brought an eerie touch of South America to the room.

Very slowly she reached out a finger and touched the jewel, then pushed it to one side as she got up from the bed. When Andrew was tucked in beneath the mosquito netting she came back, and picked the beautiful thing up. Nicholas watched her through heavy-lidded eyes, his mouth compressed and grim.

'Put it on me,' she said huskily, and turned her back to him, brushing her curls forward to leave the vulnerable nape of her neck bare.

His fingers barely touched her skin, but she shivered as she faced him.

'How does it look?' she asked.

Anger glittered in his glance and there was a pallor around his mouth that warned her she was pushing him very close to the edge. He didn't so much as glance at the necklace; from beneath a frown his gaze was fixed on her as though he would like to hurt her.

She knew a moment's fear before he said slowly, thickly, 'Like you. Beautiful, making no concessions, setting its own standards.'

And she knew, those suspicions hardened now into

certainty. For a moment triumph surged within her, glowing in her eyes, pulling her mouth into a small smile. And then in the full surge of its strength it ebbed and died and she could feel the sour taste clogging her throat.

Her hands came up to her face as she crumpled into tears, shattering, difficult tears which hurt her chest and throat, tearing through the small slenderness of her body with the impact of a series of blows.

For a moment Nicholas let her weep alone until she strained her arms about her midriff and stumbled towards the bed. Then his arms enclosed her in a grip so fierce that she winced. It did not relax. He said shakenly, 'Don't cry, my darling. Oh, God, don't cry. You're free to go now, whenever you want to. Please— don't cry.'

But the tensions built up through the long months took a long time to dissipate, and finally when the tears faded and dried she was lying against him exhausted, her face pressed into the bosom of his shirt, listening dreamily to the heavy thump of his heart.

'All right?' he asked.

She nodded, hiccuping slightly, and he sat her down on the side of the bed and left her, emerging from the bathroom with a face flannel and a towel.

'I must look awful,' she muttered, accepting them with gratitude.

'Mmm. Rather puffy about the eyes.'

He spoke in his usual controlled, slightly sardonic voice, but when she looked at him his eyes revealed the incredible truth. They dwelt on her face with a kind of naked craving which brought a stain of colour to her skin, and the hand which brushed the heavy mass of curls away from her damp forehead trembled as it moved.

'So what do we do now?' he asked. 'Dare I hope

that you're not going to exult in your triumph as you deserve to?'

Alannah sighed, understanding now so many things. 'I'm not very different from those other women you've wooed and won,' she said, making the only gesture that would satisfy them both. If she left him he would make no effort to win her back; what was needed now was the melting surrender which warmed her whole being. 'Only I promise you that money has nothing to do with it.'

A lean finger tipped her chin. He drew a deep breath as he saw the sweet submission in her face and asked very quietly, his voice totally at variance with the leaping lights in his eyes, 'Are you very sure, Alannah? Because I won't be content with your body, though I think I might die if I never lose myself in your fiery sweetness again. I want all of you. Heart, body and soul, mine for all time.'

'Oh, I'm sorry,' she choked. 'Why do you think I fought you so fiercely? Because I knew that if I gave even an inch you'd take me over completely. I fought for my independence, and when you gave it back to me I realised that the only freedom I want is the freedom of your heart.'

His finger traced the outline of her mouth, moved to the slender line of her throat and shoulder. 'No half measures with you, are there?' he whispered. 'When you hate you hate with everything in you. Will it be the same in love, Alannah?'

'Why not see?' she invited, taking courage from the age-old spell unwinding between them.

He shook his head, the dark lashes hiding his thoughts. 'Not just sex, although I find a continual delight in your body. That's no longer enough.'

'It's a good start,' she whispered, taking his hand to hold it against the warm swell of her breast.

He moved so swiftly that she was borne back

among the pillows before she had time to think, gasping as his mouth came down on hers in a kiss that annihilated time and space.

'Torment,' he groaned after an aeon, 'you tantalising little witch—I should have run like hell the first day I saw you instead of deciding to marry you.'

She lifted heavy lids to survey the taut, driven hunger in his face. 'But you love me,' she said, failing entirely to hide the satisfaction in her voice.

'Oh, yes,' he vowed. And later, 'So much, so much! I thought I could take you and mould you into a reasonable wife, that you'd be reasonably happy. The first time we met I felt that basic attraction, so I wasn't worried about any lack of response in you.'

Alannah tipped her head back, frowning. 'But that was when—you were mourning for Ngaire. You couldn't have noticed me like that.'

'No?' he smiled fiercely, and touched his mouth to her shoulder, his lips moving against the warm skin as he spoke. 'I'll admit that I was in shock. I loved Ngaire—oh, not like this—this all-consuming emotion I feel for you—but she was sweet and gentle and she depended entirely on me. I grieved deeply for her. And a month after her death I met a redheaded little sixteen-year-old who stared at me as if I were the devil and enraged me by giggling once she thought she was safely out of earshot. And this little traitor in your throat throbbed and throbbed while the air between us fairly sparked with sexual tension.'

His mouth covered the betraying pulse as he whispered, 'And I wanted to take her into my bedroom and strip her and make myself master of that slender young body. Why else do you think I schemed to get you completely in my power?'

Her eyes were wide with astonishment. 'I don't believe you!'

'No? Then why did I deliberately set out to entrap your father into risking his money?'

Her withdrawal was instinctive and palpable; across her back his arm tightened. Alannah watched as the lines of his face sharpened to make him once more the man who had forced her into marriage.

'Because that's exactly what I did,' he said harshly, making her face again the dark side of his character. 'Quite deliberately and with only one thing in mind, to put you in a position where you would have to accept me as a husband. Only, and please, my darling, believe this, although I meant to allow you no escape, I didn't mean you to be unhappy.' A cynical smile twisted his lips. 'I'm everything you've ever called me, but I'm not a monster. I truly thought that you'd be as happy as it was in you to be.'

'Conceit!' she teased, pressing little kisses along the ruthless line of his jaw. Within her the heat was building, inducing a certain languor in her limbs and body. Half beneath him, she absorbed with every sense his physical presence so that she seemed a receptacle for him, soaking up his weight, the scent and texture of his skin, the heat from his body and the sound of his breathing, the tattoo of his heart against hers.

'Probably.' Nicholas looked down into her teasing face with a rueful expression. 'Oh, almost certainly, but most men with money will tell you that it's not difficult to buy almost any woman you want. And I'd be a fool if I didn't know that I have something most women want.'

'It's called sexual magnetism,' she whispered into his ear. 'And you're no fool.'

The dark head bowed, came to rest on her breasts. He began to toy with the thin yellow stuff of her bikini bra, little sensuous movements that stopped her breath in her throat.

'A year ago I'd have said just that,' he agreed

soberly, sliding a finger between the bikini and her skin. 'Only then I didn't realise that a little schoolgirl with a will of iron and a nice line in contempt could make a fool of me.'

Only his finger moved in subtle little caresses which were driving her crazy. It had been so long since that last wild coming together. Deep inside Alannah could feel that inexorable tension growing, but this time there would be no resisting it. This time she would give of herself with complete abandon.

'If I hadn't thought I was in love with David I might have surrendered much sooner,' she said, her voice husky in her throat.

The tormenting little caress stopped. Nicholas replaced his finger with his mouth and even through the bikini the searing touch made her stomach contract in a spasm of desire.

'Damned David,' he said, self-mockery colouring the deep tones. 'I was jealous, of course, bitterly sexually jealous.' He sighed and lifted his head, looking deep into her eyes. 'That cool disdain was like a red rag to a bull. I'd expected to initiate a shy virgin; instead I was allowed to do what I wanted to a passive, uninvolved body. It was about as rewarding as making love to a doll, and it left me with a very nasty taste in my mouth. You refused to submit except in the most basic way, and that wasn't enough. And you were obviously bitterly unhappy and resentful.'

'So you became as cruel as you could be.' She understood now.

He nodded, and for long moments just held her gently and protectively, his cheek resting on her tumbled curls. 'I should have known then,' he said.

Alannah slid a finger between his shirt front and his chest and began to undo a button, revelling in the sudden hardening of his body. It pleased her to lose herself in the sight and feel of him; the years ahead, so

suddenly full of promise, would bring them emotional
and mental fulfilment, but at the moment she had a lot
of physical delights to catch up on, and now was an
excellent time to begin.

'You're asking for trouble,' Nicholas said thickly as
she ran her small hands over his shoulders, sensuously
enjoying the smooth warmth of his skin over muscles
which were strong and tense.

She laughed softly in her throat, looking up at him
through her lashes. It was exciting to flirt with him.
'Well, no, trouble is not what I'm asking for.'

'Can we?' he asked deeply.

Nodding, she said, 'Dr Stewart said this morning
that we can resume marital relations.'

'Is that what we do?' He laughed with teasing
tenderness and pulled her hard against him, letting her
feel how passion transfigured him.

At the sudden tremor which shook her he smiled
and bent his head and gently bit the side of her neck,
the touch of his teeth sending shivers of delight
through her.

'Are you seducing me?' she asked.

'I think I must be—although it's most improper for
a man to seduce his wife of almost a year.' Deep in the
green eyes little gold fires were kindling, hot, as
devouring as the mouth that was tasting the slender
fragility of her throat.

Alannah found herself making gasping little sounds
at the drowsy, desirous tide of sensation that was
rushing higher and higher, submerging her in its
force. Her hands on his body became fierce, matching
the swiftness with which he despatched her bikini top.
Moving with slow finesse his hands traced the
contours of her breasts, then slipped to the ties which
held the rest of her bikini in place.

His gentle caresses tormented her when her body
cried out for his strength and complete domination.

After he had flicked the ties free his mouth touched the hips which had cradled his child; she ran her fingers through the thick dark hair and without realising it, unable to hear her voice through the mad drumming of her heart in her ears, began to plead with him.

'Tell me you love me,' he demanded, moving so that he loomed over her, his lips only a fraction away from hers.

'I love you—I love you with everything I am. Nick—please——'

'And that you want me.' He was merciless, his expression so ferociously controlled that for a moment she was afraid.

'You know——'

'*Tell me!*'

'Oh, please, I want you.' Tears glazed her eyes. She was hypnotised by her own sensuality. Twisting, writhing beneath him, she slid her hands to his hips, pulling him down to her. 'I love you so much I could die for you,' she groaned.

'It's only a little death,' he said, quite calmly.

Then his breathing became laboured as he cast free from that intense restraint. He muttered husky endearments, words of passion such as she had never dreamed of, and she gasped as their bodies fused together in an explosion of rapture so intense that when it was over they lay exhausted in each other's arms while outside their room the sun beat towards the west, and the estuary came back to life after the heat of the day.

It was Alannah who spoke first, her voice awed as she lifted her head from his chest. 'If I'd had any idea that it could be like that I don't think I'd have had the strength to resist you so strongly.'

'There speaks the complete sensualist,' he jeered, the ice in his eyes gone for ever as they lovingly surveyed her flushed face. 'Why do you think you maddened me so much? I knew that there were other fires about you besides your hair.'

'Is that why you decided not to—to take me after that last time?'

'Mmm, partly.' He kissed her long and lingeringly, smiling at her sweet, abandoned response. 'Plus a guilty conscience. Also self-disgust.' He rolled on to his back, scooping her with him so that he could see her face above him.

'And . . .' she prompted, running a tender finger over the strong bones of his face.

His lips twitched. 'I rather hoped you'd miss my attentions. Now call me conceited again!'

Alannah's answering smile was roguish; it faded and she bent to kiss where her finger had gone, light little kisses punctuating her query. 'How well do you know Caroline Sterling? Don't answer that if you don't want to.'

'I don't mind in the least,' Nicholas returned blandly, bringing up his hands to frame her face. 'I took her out several times before we were married. I kissed her—oh, once or twice. I told her once that she was very beautiful, which you must admit she is. And when she flew to Melbourne with Ralph and me it was purely her own idea. Were you jealous?'

'You beast, you know perfectly well I was madly jealous,' she admitted, smiling because it all seemed so silly now.

'So you made sure she had to go to the ball alone.'

She lifted her eyes from their intense contemplation of his chin. He was smiling, mockery—tender mockery, creasing his cheeks.

'Well, only partly,' she confessed shamefacedly. 'I did have a backache, but it almost went away. You could have gone.'

Laughing, he kissed her until she was rosy and hotcheeked. 'Devious, aren't you? I had my suspicions, and how I prayed that I was right. It was almost the first hopeful sign that you'd given me! When did you know you loved me, dearest heart?'

'When I was having Andrew I wanted you—oh, very much! I felt that if you were with me nothing could go wrong. But I didn't realise that I loved you until you told me I could take Andrew and go, this afternoon, and I knew then that you must love me. And instead of feeling triumphant I could only cry.'

'Defiant to the end! If you wanted me there when you were in labour why did you dream of David Opie after you came home?'

'I think it must have been a renunciation, my subconscious telling me what I'd refused to accept.' Seriously she told him about the dream.

'It almost cut my heart out,' Nicholas said with sombre intensity, pulling her head down on to his shoulder. His voice was very deep as he continued, 'I realised then that I'd have to confront you with him. You had the right to choose. But I was terrified that you'd decide on him. The prospect of a life without you filled me with terror.'

'*Terror?*' Astounded, she lifted her head, saw confirmation in the taut mask of his features. 'Oh, darling!' she breathed, and wound her arms around him, hugging him to her with all of her strength. 'Darling you must have realised—you're experienced enough to——'

'Oh, yes, experience is one thing I have in plenty,' he agreed harshly. 'And what the hell use was it to me? I knew you wanted me, but you were so cold, so icily resentful. Whenever we made love you suffered my touch as though it degraded you. And I was falling deeper and deeper in love with you——'

'When?'

His breath ruffled the curls at her temple. 'Oh, right

from the start. I knew when I came on you in the bathroom the day Stewart confirmed your pregnancy. You were a charming shade of green and your little face was pinched and wan. I wanted to pick you up and hold you against my heart for the rest of our lives. You looked like an exhausted child, and I felt a heel.'

'And I spat poison at you,' she sighed regretfully, turning her head to kiss his shoulder.

A faint noise from the crib made her stiffen. It sounded as though Andrew was going through the complicated procedure that denoted his awakening, little grunts which came closer and closer together. With a different sort of sigh, though just as regretful, she pulled away from Nicholas's clasp and ran across to get a wrap from the dressing room.

When she came back in she looked at her husband, magnificent in unembarrassed nudity on the big bed, his hands clasped behind his head as he watched her, relaxed, almost complacent.

'Like a Greek statue,' she teased, smiling, her eyes large and very brilliant as she bent to kiss his shoulder. 'A very sexy Greek statue. With a hungry son.'

He grinned at her. 'And a very sexy wife. Are you going to nurse him like that?'

'Why not? He's too young to realise that I've no clothes on underneath. Do you think I should dress?'

Nicholas slid a hand beneath the wrap, pushing back the material so that he could kiss the golden skin of her thigh. 'No, it hardly seems worthwhile. Not when I'll have to take them all off again afterwards.'

Alannah's vivid blush made her look like a schoolgirl, but her response was purely adult. 'I've always heard that your average Greek god was practically insatiable when it came to his appetites, especially sex. I'm inclined to believe it.'

His soft, satisfied laughter followed her across the room. And afterwards, when they had loved each other again and swum and showered, they sat out on their bedroom terrace waiting for Rose to come home from her day on the yacht.

Curled up on Nicholas's lap, Alannah asked soberly, 'Will we always be as happy as this?'

'Yes,' he said promptly, tightening his arm about her. 'This is only the beginning, my heart, this rapture. As for anything else—well, we have the only security this world can give. We're both survivors.' His eyes crinkled as they swept the earnest, adoring face lifted to his. 'As we damned well needed to be,' he taunted softly. 'You've led me one hell of a dance, my beloved, quick-witted, proud, bad-tempered termagant. If I'd had less stamina I'd have packed everything in months ago.'

Her arms wound around his shoulders as she kissed the spot where the proud column of his neck met his shoulder, her lips moving with sensuous purpose over the fine tanned skin.

'Would you?' she asked sweetly, touching her tongue to the place where his heartbeat thudded and began to pick up speed.

'No.' Deep in his throat he laughed, and slid his hand from her hip to the warm, rounded curve of her breast. 'Never, my lovely. I need you to make me happy.'

Alannah stopped her caressing and tilted her head back to look at him. 'I love you,' she whispered, 'Darling, darling, darling. . . .'

Locked together in a swift resurgence of passion, they kissed and kissed once more, and Alannah knew the incandescent magic of his touch. Yet deeper and stronger was the delight caused by the knowledge of Nicholas's love. So dearly won, so little sought, but her future happiness was based entirely on this mixture of respect and affection and desire, this complete surrender to each other.

There would be other moments of pure joy in their lives, but none so fresh as this, now that her guarded heart was at last open to his possession. This was all she had ever desired.